I, VILLAIN

© 2017 Marcus V. Calvert

By Tales Unlimited, LLC.

All rights reserved.

For permissions, contact:
https://squareup.com/store/TANSOM.

Cover by Lincoln Adams

Edited by Ed Buchanan

To Madison!

Enjoy the Mayhem.

Marcus V. Calvert

9-30-17

ACKNOWLEDGEMENTS

I'd like to thank Ed Buchanan (my editor) for his expertise, steady support, and blunt-force candor.

I'd also like to thank Lincoln Adams (my cover artist) for his time, patience, and wicked-awesome skill.

Rose, thanks for keeping me in the game.

To everyone else who had a hand in this twisted thing being written (living or not), I thank you.

I must also tip a hat to my fellow artists and strangers-turned-fans. You truly are a hip crowd.

CHAPTER ONE

I sat alone in a corner booth and scowled at my half-empty glass of white wine. Here, in the *Versantio Hotel's* main ballroom, two hundred-plus Irish mobsters and their dates ate, drank, and partied. While the O'Flernans celebrated, I stewed over why they made my life a thousand times more difficult.

They had broken one of my cardinal rules: *No children, no feds.*

I didn't mind making new enemies. It's a side effect of my business. But tonight's little soiree might get me arrested, killed, or worse.

I'm a fixer. My job's to make other people's problems go away. If the money's right, I arrange miracles. I've got killers, thieves, forgers, and super villains on my payroll. My firm's worked cases on both sides of the law and in every corner of the world. I've had innocent people rescued. I've had innocent people killed. After ten-plus years in the trade, I rarely got my hands bloody anymore. But I don't have any illusions about who I am.

I'm the bad guy: plain and simple.

My reputation varied, depending on the organization. The O'Flernans, for example, loved my work. Law enforcement agencies despised me . . . until they needed a messy job done "off-the-books." In Mockre's case, the potential loss of government clientele wasn't an issue. What bothered me were the odds that—after tonight—I'd be featured on a black ops kill list.

I glanced over at *Iron Sweat.* The band was in the middle of some quirky rock piece. Too talented to be playing this faux Irish wake, the six-person band ruled their modest rectangular stage. A few dozen couples danced before them, caught up in the sway of strong booze and rhythmic tunes. My eyes drifted over to

Vincent Mockre's coffin. It wasn't set in a position of honor. No, the coffin was just behind the stage, vertically-mounted on the wall like a perverse hunting trophy.

Made of polished silver, the coffin had a transparent, airtight lid. Inside was Agent Vincent Mockre (possibly of the FBI, DEA, U.S. Customs, or God-knows-what-other agency). He was about to die tonight because someone blew his cover.

I was that someone.

The O'Flernans came to me about a month ago. They smelled something "wrong" about Mockre. They were nervous because he was one of their most trusted enforcers. He knew plenty of their secrets and had access to all of their local operations. The O'Flernans wanted to know if he had been tempted (or forced) to sell them out.

Unable to figure it out themselves, they approached me. I tasked two of my best teams to trail him night-and-day. At first, nothing was out of place. Mockre didn't appear to have a handler or partners in the field. All of his personal dealings, calls, and e-mails appeared on the up-and-up (for a crook, anyway).

It took three weeks before Mockre fucked up and led us right to his safe house. When he left, my teams discreetly breached and discovered his gear. He had a complex surveillance suite set up in the dining room, complete with server. At some point, he had planted bugs and hidden cameras throughout every O'Flernan-owned location in town. When my contractors took his gear away—for analysis—it almost instantly self-destructed. Given time, we might've figured out Mockre's employer but the O'Flernans wanted their "leak" plugged.

They snatched him up the next day.

Once they paid me, I could've just walked away . . . which wasn't how I worked. Unfinished jobs bothered me. I had my best data sifters and psi-hackers tear into Mockre's background again in the hopes that something new might emerge. There was another reason I wanted to know who owned his ass. If he was running black ops for the CIA or NSA, blowing his cover might get me killed.

I figured that Mockre's people would try to save him—either directly or indirectly. The direct approach would call for a massive federal raid. This event would be a wet dream for any law enforcement agency. If I were a senior fed, I'd personally bust in here with a hundred-plus agents at my back. In the process of rescuing my dying undercover, I'd arrest everyone else in the room. Anyone who even looked at me wrong would get double-tapped between the eyes. When I showed Mockre's mangled face to the media, I'd probably be labeled a hero and offered a book deal.

Or, perhaps, his extraction would be more indirect. A small team of elite operatives could figure out a way to get around these Irish felons and retrieve their boy. Such an operation required skill sets, planning, super powers, and the right gear. Whether or not they succeeded, their methods would leave me enough "fingerprints" to identify them.

Either way, Mockre's extraction team had better hurry. He wasn't going to last much longer. Once upon a time, the tall, muscular superhuman could've called himself handsome. Now, his face was a ruined mess. While his gray suit looked okay from a darkened distance, we all knew better. Up-close, his clothes were ripped and blood-soaked.

Aside from being locked in the air-tight coffin, Mockre's wrists and legs were bound by standard-issue prison shackles. A string of white, blinking Christmas lights was wrapped around his neck and torso. The ghoulish touch made him a focal point in the dimly lit room.

About an hour ago, four O'Flernan soldiers dragged him out, shackles and all. Beforehand, Mockre was sprayed with inhibitor serum. A single 12-hour dose would neutralize his super strength, flight abilities, and bulletproof skin. Until it wore off, he was just a regular guy with a lot of breakable bones.

Worse, the stuff did nothing to dull his pain.

The guests parted, while showering Mockre with curses, confetti, and spit. Judging from his bruises, someone had already worked him over—but that was just foreplay. After they kicked the banquet hall staff out of the room, they actually let *Iron Sweat* stick around and watch.

What came next was a private matter.

A gray folding chair was set out at the center of the dance floor. We gathered around as Mockre was thrown into it. His former colleagues happily laid into the half-conscious traitor with brass knuckles, baseball bats, and even chains. Everyone else cheered during the rage-filled beat down—even the band.

The rest of the O'Flernans enjoyed every punch, every blunt-force impact, and every agonized moan that came from Mockre's busted mouth. Some even whistled and applauded like drunken football fans. Mockre was coughing up blood after three minutes and unconscious in five. However, he did manage to scream when they cut his tongue out and cauterized what was left.

Behind him, six O'Flernan "pall bearers" brought out the coffin and stuffed Mockre into it: barely alive and still conscious. I looked around for a squeamish or sympathetic face but none of these hard-cased felons fit that mold. As far as they were concerned, Mockre had betrayed the "family" and deserved whatever he got. As for backup, I should've known better. No one was coming to save this guy.

Luckily, I had an extraction plan.

While the O'Flernans were long-time clients, I wasn't dumb enough to fuck with Uncle Sam. Diligent investigators could find out how Mockre died. When they did, I'm sure my name would come up as being involved. So, I called in some of my shiftier contractors. Together, we planned a rescue op for the poor idiot.

Dressed as banquet hall staff, my people had served spiked drinks to the O'Flernan mobsters all night. Our chemical of choice was both non-lethal and slow acting. By my estimates, it would kick in within the next thirty minutes. The targets would sleep all night and not remember the last 12 hours or so.

Everyone imbibed some by now, whether they were into whiskey shots or glasses of ginger ale. Hell, I imagine the substance even found its way into our catered meals. That was the way my team worked. Soon, the mob guests would all drop—even me. And the O'Flernans (when they woke up) would blame it all on Mockre's mysterious employer(s). My people would get Mockre out of here and heal him up. By the time my telepaths were done, he wouldn't remember the last two years of his life—but he'd have a tongue again.

Fair trade, I'd say.

The only thing was that Mockre might not be a fed after all. Being abandoned like this hinted that he didn't belong to any of the major agencies. Also, he might work for a rival organization or as a foreign operative. The guy might even be a solo act. Hopefully, my team could figure that out tonight.

Pinpoint walked up with a glass of white wine on her tray. At twenty-eight, she was tall, slim, and packed the sweetest smile. Her cute face was intelligent and deceptively harmless. She had fair, freckled skin and dark brown hair tied into a ponytail. Her server uniform consisted of black shoes and slacks, with a white jacket over her white blouse. Her black bow tie was a bit crooked, which was probably an intentional touch. As I sized up her uniform, I wondered how many guns she packed right now.

Some supers could bench-press buildings or run faster than sound. Pinpoint had a natural mastery of any firearm. Not interested in being a cop or a spy, she bounced around the world as a soldier-of-fortune.

Eighteen months ago, the gal simply appeared on my doorstep and asked if I was hiring. Amused, I gave her a list of 12 locals: all low-level crooks with bounties. Individually, they weren't worth my time. But as a package deal, their bounties would add up to a decent sum. Rather than send a team, I sent her. Pinpoint's job interview was to kill them all in three days.

She finished in two.

Once I confirmed the kills, I was so impressed that I let her keep half of the bounty cash as a hiring bonus. Pinpoint's slaughtered for me—without a qualm—ever since.

"Care for a refill, sir?" Pinpoint asked.

"Please," I replied with a smile.

She slipped a white paper napkin in front of me, with a handwritten message in neat Mandarin: *Blank on both fronts. Abort?*

Shit.

"Both fronts" referred to figuring out Mockre's true identity and retrieving any useful intel left in his brain. If my psi-hackers still hadn't found any holes in his background, then it wasn't a fake. While he might've been a snitch, Vincent Mockre wasn't a federal agent or working with some kind of alias.

Stranger still, my best telepaths couldn't get into his head.

The O'Flernans worked on Mockre over the last five days. I would've expected their telepaths to have crushed through the man's psychic defenses (if any) by now. His mind—what was left of it—should've been easy pickings. Someone must've fitted him with high-end mental defenses (either psychic or technological) that even my people couldn't crack.

Oh well . . .

I looked up at Pinpoint and gave her a discreet nod, confirming my order to abort. She looked disappointed. Frankly, I didn't have a choice. Without more intel, it wasn't worth the risk of saving Mockre. Besides, maybe he had it coming.

Pinpoint set the full glass down on top of her message, and then gestured toward my half-empty one.

"Want me to take your glass?"

"Not yet," I replied. "But thank you."

She gave me a friendly nod and walked away. My people would work the room for the rest of the event. During that time, they'd release the counteragent. Colorless and odorless, the gas would negate the effects of the chemical in the drinks.

In the end, any O'Flernan who passed out would only be able to blame the booze.

CHAPTER TWO

The evening wore on with Mockre slowly dying in the background. I was interrupted halfway through my late-evening e-mails.

"Come with us, Mr. Cly," a male voice shouted over the band.

I looked up from my smartphone. Three large men towered over my booth, all dressed in black suits. The "chatty" one stood in the middle and looked to be in charge of the hard-faced trio.

They weren't human.

I could spot superhumans—and their powers—at a glance. A useful ability, it revealed that all three were quite dangerous.

The leader was a kinetic.

To his left was a metalformer.

The one on the kinetic's right was a pyrokinetic . . . of sorts.

Hired for their offensive abilities, these dark-haired "lads" looked Irish enough to be here tonight—not that it mattered. When it came to hiring superhumans, Seamus didn't care about ethnicity. If a potential recruit had useful powers and played by the O'Flernans' rules, that super was always welcomed. Openness like that gave the O'Flernans an edge over the other local mobs, which still preferred their ethnic ties.

Still, this didn't seem right.

Normally, Seamus' bodyguards were human—which made sense. I wouldn't pay my superhuman contractors to babysit me either. My people were more valuable in the field, solving problems for well-paying clients. Previously, whenever Seamus wanted to meet, he'd send one of his rank-and-file to fetch me. Now, I was looking at three heavy-hitters.

It wasn't his style.

Either he was worried about a specific threat or this was the rescue op I had been anticipating all night. These three could be federal agents, trying to lure me into a late-night incarceration—or worse. My people would be watching. If things got too far out of line, then they could intervene. Since I had been expecting to get caught up in a federal raid, extraction plans were in place.

Too bad those plans were worthless now.

These guys had singled me out, which we didn't account for. Yes, my people could adapt and still attempt a rescue. The problem was that, with the exception of Pinpoint, their skill sets and powers were suited for stealth. These three could easily wipe out my entire team—and half the building—if things got violent.

An irritated sigh escaped my lips as I polished off my second glass of wine. Then I slid out of my booth and put the phone away. The kinetic took point and headed for the nearest exit. The other two waited for me to follow and then formed up on either side of me. These three drew curious stares from the rank-and-file mobsters, which made me doubt that they were O'Flernans.

We passed Vincent Mockre's coffin. I would've sworn that the poor bastard was still moving around a bit. My "escorts" utterly ignored the traitor, which could've meant that they weren't here to save him. I noticed Pinpoint, who stepped away from a crowded table, plates of food in hand. She gave me her "I-hope-you-know-what-you're-doing" frown and then went back to work.

If this was business, I'd handle it. Trouble? I'd handle that as well.

We headed out into the hallway and toward a bank of elevators: three on each side. The metalformer tapped a button and kept his eyes on me. The natural-born super stayed within arm's reach, which made sense. In the blink of an eye, his pale body could turn into solid titanium. His skin, internal organs, and even his hair would become metal. As for physical strength, I suspect that he could punt me across the city without much effort.

His partners eyed either end of the hallway with the lethal readiness of professional muscle. I gave their powers a second glance and felt a bit envious. The kinetic's eye beams were a straightforward part of his augmentation. The fact that he could make energy shapes—from said eye beams—was even more intriguing.

The pyrokinetic's power was a minor birth defect. A natural-born super, he should've been able to create and control flames with his mind alone. Instead, his power had an oral component. With a bit of concentration, his voice could cause objects to burst into psychic flame (which he couldn't control or douse). Still, the louder he talked, the bigger the fire—which made him dangerous enough.

The nearest elevator door had a nice steel polish to it. Since I was about to see the big man, I used this opportunity to check myself over. There was confetti on the left shoulder of my navy-blue Armani knockoff, which I quickly brushed away. I've worn this same armored suit almost every day for damned-near ten years. It survived shootings, bombings, and plenty of other hazardous events while looking just as new as the day it was made.

Armor was a necessity in my line of work but it had to be subtler than, say, a suit of plate mail. Thus, my ten pounds of grenade-proof, multi-functional business attire was a logical choice. Layered with armored nanofibers, my suit was worth more than this entire building. Even as I picked up love handles over the years, the suit self-tailored for a relaxed fit. The white shirt and black shoes were also part of the package.

Satisfied with my clothing, I gave my face a quick once-over.

I needed some tanning bed time. Brutishly ugly with a decent chin, my lifestyle (surprisingly) didn't make me look much older than my forty-three years. I stroked the thick brownish-gray goatee. A month-old, it itched a bit but folks seemed to like me better with one. I noticed some bits of confetti in my slicked-back hair. Since I didn't have a comb, I didn't bother dealing with it. Then I sized up my gray eyes and waited for a twinge of revulsion, guilt, or self-loathing.

I had just watched a man get beaten, mutilated, and left to die in a coffin. To my relief, I didn't give a shit. I had seen—and done—much worse in my past. Being a decent fixer required a clinical detachment that bordered on lunacy.

Even mobsters cared about someone. True fixers, however, could only care about their own lives, business interests, and reputations. Period. Things like conscience, family, and friends were merely exploitable weaknesses.

The elevator door opened. I stepped in first. The trio followed, eyes locked on me. As the doors closed, the metalformer signaled me to raise my arms. I gave him an understanding grin, complied, and waited for the frisk. Still, if these clowns crossed a line, I'd have to kill them (even if they were feds or mobsters). In an enclosed elevator, I actually had good odds. Still, we'd make quite a mess.

The metalformer professionally frisked me and took my pair of Glock .40's from their holsters. I kept them together, at the small of my back. While I didn't like guns, I liked being shot even less. He pulled the pair of spare mags from my suit jacket's inner pockets. Then he tucked them into his own suit and signaled me to lower my arms.

The kinetic tapped the top floor button and up we went.

Not a word was spoken, which was fine by me. Whether this was just business or a clever ambush, at least I got out of that goddamned party. After my chat with Seamus (or whoever), I'd be back out on the streets doing what I did best. I glanced at my watch. It was twenty-two minutes past eleven on a Friday night. After this, I'd pay my contractors for tonight's work, grab a bite, and prep for my one o'clock with Grace Lexia.

I was surprised when Grace called and told me that she was back in town. After *Clean Sweep*, that wasn't such a bright idea. The last time I checked, the average kill bounty on her head was in the low seven figures. While I could've set her up and collected that bounty, I chose not to.

Since she had gone into hiding (again), Grace was still a living legend among psi-hackers—arguably the best. Over the last year, I'd hear the occasional gossip about her exploits. Almost once a month, Grace would target a crook and steal his/her digital life savings. The money would then be donated to charity or simply disappear. Other times, Grace would get wind of a serious terror plot and tip off the authorities.

In a world without super heroes, she was the next best thing.

If it weren't for her scruples, I'd have put Grace on my payroll. Hell, she would've been in charge of the Mockre case—and good enough to figure out why he was snooping on his fellow mobsters. Depending on what Grace needed tonight, I might put her to that task— as payment for my services.

The gal must be in a real jam to come back.

Pillar City was often thought of as a "Sodom and Gomorrah sandwich" because it was two corrupt boroughs on one artificial island. Uptown was the sea-level metropolis with all the urban perks of nearby Manhattan (only cheaper). The streets were cleaner and safer. The officials preached about honest politics, avoided scandals, and still managed to get their kickbacks. If I had to raise kids in Pillar City, I suppose Uptown would've been suitable.

But I rarely spent time there.

Below Uptown's sewers was Downtown. Easily the crime capital of the U.S., it was a mixture of slums and busy industrial zones. For eleven years, I've lived down here and enjoyed its thin veneer of morality. Here, everyone had price tags on their corrupted souls. The path to power wasn't that hard to find—as long as you were smart enough and amoral enough to walk it.

Anywhere else, a place this decadent would've ended up in an economic shitfall with fleeing businesses and abundant cases of political neglect. Instead, Downtown is a thriving urban hell. The secret to its success was one simple rule: take care of the city and it'll take care of you.

To that end, the powers-that-be never allowed inept governance in either half of Pillar City. Instead, they made it a money-making wonderland. Over the decades, criminals (like myself) flocked here and brought cash with them. Even legitimate businesses—once they bribed the right people—could make solid fortunes. There were fewer regulatory hassles, solid Downtown infrastructure, and easy access to Uptown's international ports.

Grace didn't share my awe of Pillar City.

Somehow, she grew up on these rough streets without losing her moral compass. As an adult, Grace didn't want to leave. Instead, she became a cop and wasted fourteen good years of her life trying to clean up Downtown's roughest neighborhoods. While she was a brilliant detective, her style was too blunt for her superiors. Also, Grace made the mistake of being an honest cop. In a way, getting blown up was probably the best thing that ever happened to her.

Her small Downtown house was bombed in '03. Back then, I had set up shop and was plugged in with the local crime scene. Word on the street was that some of her fellow cops planted the bomb to keep Grace off a high-profile murder case. Apparently, the main suspect was both guilty as hell and very rich. When he felt pressured by Grace, he paid some of Pillar City's finest to make the case go away—by any means necessary.

Grace ended up in a burn ward, comatose and minus her legs. Her insurance wouldn't pay enough for a healer. Her doctors had been bribed to advise her gullible sister to pull the plug. Five minutes after the plug was yanked, Grace woke up. She quit the force that day. When she was well enough to travel, Grace left the city and fell off the grid. Life went on and Grace Lexia was all but forgotten.

Then, in '05, she came back home.

Healed from head-to-toe, the former cop had (somehow) hooked up with The Outfitter, Pillar City's number one gadget and weapons maker. Strictly freelance, he was a natural-born super genius who had outfitted villains for over twenty years. Like most crooks in this town, I was a loyal client because he made some awesome shit.

One day, I showed up at his shop, which was concealed under a 24-hour dry cleaner. While waiting for The Outfitter, I glanced over at Grace, who worked the counter for about half her old salary.

What I saw almost made me run away.

Grace's mind was amped. In fact, it was souped up to a level that was beyond frightening. A ball of angst had somehow manifested as a raw form of psi-hacking. It wasn't an augment or a natural ability. This was something raging and powerful enough to make one's head explode.

Somehow, it didn't killer her. My guess was that The Outfitter had put an implant or two in her head. Since my ability to assess organic powers couldn't spot tech-based implants, I could only guess. The arrangement between them was simple enough to figure out. The Outfitter had placed her under his protection. In exchange, she managed his shop and psi-hacked for him. Back then, she kept her talent under wraps.

After his death in 2011, word got out that The Outfitter had been secretly aiding hero groups—with both op tech and intel. This revelation upset a lot of his former clients (myself included).

With The Outfitter gone, Grace Lexia was seen as a nice consolation prize. As the only surviving link to The Outfitter and what he knew, some of her enemies wanted her alive. But more of them didn't. Grace knew that the longer she was on these streets, the higher that price on her head. Once again, she wisely fled town.

I couldn't wait to find out what made her come back.

The elevator doors opened onto the thirty-first floor. Out we stepped. I took point while the others flanked my sides and rear. In front of me was a narrow hallway, which opened out into the *Versantio Hotel's* four-star rooftop restaurant. Normally packed with aging snobs, the restaurant had been bought out for tonight's festivities. The eatery overlooked most of the Downtown skyline, which stretched for miles in all directions.

While the skyline wasn't too special, the sky itself was.

I looked up at the holographic night. Some German super geniuses designed Downtown's synthetic weather system in the late 1800's to boost citizen morale. The system received upgrades every few decades or so, in the quest of better imitating the outside world. While impressive, the fake sunlight, rain, and even snow could never quite measure up to the real thing. Still, it was better than looking up at a sprawling metal roof.

I strolled down the hallway, past a NO SMOKING sign. I pulled out a pack of Marlboros, put my lips around a cigarette, and slid it out. Then I put the pack away and fished for my lighter –

"Allow me," the pyrokinetic whispered.

His two words made my cigarette's tip burst into flames. I barely flinched as I kept the Marlboro between my lips. I turned and gave the pyro a thankful nod, wondering if I'd have to kill him in the next few minutes. At the far end of the restaurant was Seamus O'Flernan. I bit back a sigh of relief, grateful that a swarm of federal super agents hadn't descended upon me.

I strolled his way. The bodyguards followed.

To someone who didn't know better, Seamus resembled a benign, redheaded Santa Claus in a white suit—thick beard and all. At sixty-eight, he was quick to smile or have someone killed: depending on the situation. Seamus was one of the four major mob bosses in this town. From nothing to Irish don inside of thirty years, his local roots ran deepest.

While the other mobs came to Pillar City to expand their operations, Seamus O'Flernan carved out his smuggling empire on these very streets. Once he got big, he expanded his operations into other port cities throughout the world. Whenever contraband needed moving, crooks looked to the O'Flernans like they were FedEx.

Not bad for a mere human.

Seamus sat in front of the remnants of a sirloin steak and baked potato. A half-empty bottle of red wine was at his left. A buxom server—not one of mine—stood to his right. In her mid-30's, she wore similar colors to Pinpoint—only her uniform came with a black skirt instead of slacks. Her frame was a bit muscular, which didn't lessen her natural beauty.

One of my people should've been serving him food tonight. Instead, this unknown was here. I looked her over for powers and found none. Perhaps she was a member of Seamus' new security detail.

"Evening, m'boy!" Seamus shouted with a slight brogue as he rose to his full 5'10" height.

"Seamus," I smiled as I shook his large right hand from across the table.

The mob boss glanced over at his guys and gave them a dismissive "fuck-off" wave with his left hand. Then he sat down and gestured for me to do the same. An artificial Downtown breeze blew past some nearby party lamps but didn't touch us. Then I thought of the henchman with the kinetic powers. My guess was that he put us in a force bubble of some kind.

On a normal night, there would've been a half-dozen triggermen in the background, not that Seamus needed them. His power came from being "too useful to kill." He greased a lot of palms in this town (from politicians to the cops to the media). Before now, he didn't even fear the major intelligence services. They needed his smuggling network just as much as anyone else with contraband to move.

Of course, such arrangements had to end sometime. If Mockre had been a fed, Seamus would have every reason to be scared of a reprisal. The busty server handed him a cigar. The Irishman stuck it in his mouth and nodded toward the enforcers, who looked on from across the restaurant. She took the hint and left. For a half-second, the breeze touched us. Then nothing. Yep, we were in a force bubble.

I glanced down at my cigarette and noticed that it was half-gone. The pyro's flames unnaturally burned through the tobacco. I noticed a glass ashtray and dropped my cigarette on it.

"Thanks for sticking around," Seamus grinned my way as he fished out a gold-plated lighter.

"I figured you might want a word," I smoothly lied.

"Oh? I thought you were just sulking."

We chuckled at that as he lit up.

"You don't approve of Mockre's . . . justice?" Seamus asked as he put his lighter away.

"You needed to send a message," I shrugged. "That follows. I just believe in fewer witnesses."

"Ah," Seamus nodded, unoffended and understanding. "It's been so long since anyone's slipped an undercover into our ranks that I felt a show was in order."

"Did you get him to talk?"

The old man shook his head and sighed through a plume of smoke.

"My people say that his psi-screen's custom-made and tougher than the President's."

"You want me to find his boss?" I offered.

"Aye. And put the fucker in the ground."

"Could get ugly: especially if he really was a fed."

"Then don't leave so many witnesses," Seamus winked.

"My fee?"

Seamus gave me a knowing smile and pulled a folded slip of white paper from inside his suit. He reached over and handed it to me. On it was the dollar amount he was offering to pay me for this job. I looked at the number and its eight digits. Then him. Then the fee again.

"$92 million?" I asked with quiet disbelief.

"We have a deal then?" Seamus asked, confident of my answer.

"Hell no."

CHAPTER THREE

Seamus O'Flernan's response was that of genuine shock. Few people ever refused his offers—especially when he started throwing money around. The problem was that 92 million was just too good to be real.

I stood up with a scowl.

"Should I double it then?" he offered.

"It's a fucking setup," I scoffed as I tossed the paper aside.

"There's no threat to you or yours, lad," Seamus soothingly lied.

"Let me guess," I pondered aloud. "I take the job. I easily find your target: someone dangerous. Someone I'd never fuck with on a normal day. But since I took your money, I can't back down. Then I send my best people to do the deed. Whether they succeed or not, I end up dead . . . and none of this comes back on you."

Seamus studied me with his best poker face.

"Am I right?"

The mobster forced a deep breath to calm his next words.

"Listen to me–" Seamus began.

"My standard track-and-kill fee's about five-mil," I told him with a raised voice. "If you had doubled it, you might've suckered me. But 92 mil's way too fucking high!"

"Perhaps I could persuade you to reconsider," Seamus insisted, talking like he still had leverage.

"Not interested," I told him.

Then I casually leaned against the force bubble like it was a permanent wall. As I folded my arms, I wondered when I became expendable in the old man's eyes. I should've seen it coming. For all his charisma, Seamus O'Flernan was still a double-dealing crook. I just thought that—after all this time—he'd know better than to try and play me.

"Cly, it's not like that –" Seamus began.

"You should've picked a schmuck fixer for this one," I interrupted.

"Oh no," Seamus replied, his expression turning dead serious. "You're just the schmuck I need. Your people are good enough to see this done, Cly. The money's more than enough to justify any losses you suffer."

"$92 million is about what I'd charge to topple a small government or start an ethnic cleansing!" I snipped. "You're clearly up against someone your people can't kill."

"That's where you're wrong, lad."

"Oh really?!" I asked. "Then who do you want dead?"

Seamus gave me a mocking chuckle. "The bastards who sent Mockre!"

"Who's the mark?!" I yelled (tired of this bullshit).

Annoyed, Seamus took a thoughtful puff from his cigar.

"Ever hear of The Black Wheel?"

"No," I replied with a bothered frown. I prided myself on having files on all kinds of dangerous organizations. Many of them became eventual clients and/or targets of mine. Thus, having extensive intel came in handy.

"They're a criminal outfit," he sighed. "Think of the old-school, 'evil schemes' variety of villainous filth. Money they have. Power they have. What they really want is . . ."

Seamus let his own voice trail and shook his head with an unknowing sigh.

"They flipped Mockre?"

Seamus nodded. Maybe he was lying. Maybe he wasn't.

"They want your outfit?"

The old man looked at me like I had asked the dumbest of questions. Of course they'd want his multi-billion-dollar empire. Taking it over was sadly possible. Seamus was almost seventy. His two sons were long dead and his only surviving child, Deidre, was a spoiled-rotten party girl. If Seamus died, maybe his lieutenants would let her run things. Or maybe they'd kill her and fight over the scraps.

One bullet through the old man's skull and it could all fall to pieces.

"I don't know what they're after," Seamus lied. "Figure that out on your own, if you're inclined. Just kill the fuckers and collect the fattest payday of your natural life. The money's real! Say you'll do it and I'll put it in your coffers tonight."

That last part was true, which bothered me. I pretended to think on it. Really though, the only question left to ask was whether or not I should kill this fucker right now.

"I'll pass," I replied five seconds later.

Seamus' face slowly turned red as he rose to his feet and made a downward gesture with his right hand. I easily regained my balance as the force bubble abruptly went away.

"Lads!" Seamus shouted. "Mr. Cly seems to have forgotten who runs this town. Why don't you come over here and help him see reason?"

This should've gone his way.

Benjamin Cly's "official record" was a carefully constructed web of bullshit.

Few people knew my real history. Those who did either kept quiet or occupied shallow graves. Aside from my gaze, I barely even used my powers anymore.

Luckily, I was good enough to survive on my wits, my armor, and some decent aim. As far as anyone knew, I was simply a street fixer who lucked out and made it big. In all respects, I should've been as helpless as any other overweight businessman with graying hair and high cholesterol.

I glanced over my left shoulder just as the three enforcers shared cruel smiles amongst themselves. They casually walked over. Seamus gave me a smug grin, certain that I'd eventually see things his way. Maybe they'd slap me around a bit. Or perhaps they'd dangle me off the roof's edge for a while (that never gets old).

The metalformer grabbed me by the lapels of my suit. He stayed flesh-and-blood because he saw that Seamus didn't want my arms torn off. That was good because I ripped his metalform power while he was frisking me in the elevator. To rip a power, all I had to do was make physical contact with a living super. The big guy wouldn't notice the loss until he tried to "metal" up.

I glanced down at his open suit jacket. Inside was a shoulder-holstered Browning 9-mil with a quick-draw rig. He wasn't even wearing Kevlar! Whatever Seamus was paying these assholes, it was too much. I fought back a smile as the web of my right hand shot out between his thick arms and popped him in the trachea. My left hand grabbed his Browning and shot him twice in the stomach.

The dying metalformer staggered to his left, which blocked the pyro's line of attack. But the kinetic could see me just fine. His eyes narrowed as I sent three rounds toward his heart. Unfortunately, my shots bounced off his circular, near-invisible force wall.

"I need him alive!" Seamus shouted as the dead metalformer hit the floor.

"YOU'RE GONNA BURN FOR THAT!" the pyrokinetic angrily yelled over his dead partner.

His words caused flames to erupt from my clothing. My suit instantly reacted.

The nanofabric tightened around me. The armor "bled" out a silvery coating over my skin, just before the flames could melt my face off. Part of the armor package, the metal covered me from the soles of my feet to the hairs on my head. Anyone looking at my face would see a reflective, featureless mask: no eyes, nose, or mouth. My suit and shoes were still there, only with less nanomolecular mass. This hermetically-sealed, armored skin came with a five-hour air supply.

The armor protected me so well that I didn't even feel warm. However, these psychic flames clung like napalm. Water or foam probably wouldn't douse them. But I knew what would . . .

The Browning was starting to melt in my hand. Not wanting to waste a decent gun, I shot the pyro. Four bullets to the chest put him down quickly enough. But even after he was dead, the flames still burned! Annoyed, I dropped the ruined gun and bolted for the kinetic, right as he blasted me off my feet.

Twin, transparent beams of force erupted from his eyes and formed a giant energy fist. About the size of a vending machine, it sent me partway through a nearby wall. Worse, he poured it on with a constant stream of unblinking force. His clear intent was to turn me into a gooey smudge. My armor hardened to prevent that from happening.

Too bad I wasn't strong enough to move . . . until I tapped the metalformer's power. As I grew taller and stronger, the armor grew with me, compensating for the half-second change in size. Anyone looking at me would figure that the suit was morphing instead of me.

Still on fire, I grabbed the transparent kinetic fist with both hands and started pushing it away. He should've just had the fist grab me up and throw me off the roof (I would've). Instead, the kinetic's beam suddenly cut off.

"The hell?!" The kinetic exclaimed, freaked that I was still standing.

Unhindered, I ran toward the bodyguard as he assumed a firmer stance, like he was going to blast me with something else. I got within five feet of the kinetic's throat when he lit into me again. Instead of another fist, I got hit with a wave of kinetic energy that stopped me cold. The field looked almost watery as it wrapped around me and began to compress.

I tried to tear through it but I couldn't move. The damned field was actually strong enough to hold me in place like flypaper. The steady beams flowed from his eyes as he then glanced upward. The field followed his gaze and lifted me off the floor. My flaming armor rippled from the pressure (something I had never seen it do before). Without the metalformer's power, he might've crushed me by now.

Instead, I felt nothing.

"Why won't you die?!" the sweating kinetic yelled as he trembled from the effort.

"Don't kill him, idiot!" Seamus yelled.

The kinetic's left nostril started to bleed.

When that field came down, I'd have to kill him before he could –

Too drained from the effort, the kinetic suddenly ceased his attack. I rushed him with a massive right punch. The desperate superhuman erected another force wall between us. He had to have known that it wouldn't hold.

My burning metalformer fist smashed through the barrier like plastic wrap. The blow continued onward and went right through his heart. Seeing as I was now taller than the kinetic, the downward motion didn't send him flying away. Instead, I had to pull my fist out of his rib cage. The damned pyro's flames finally died down, leaving my white shirt scorched.

Seamus cringed as I flicked bits of dead kinetic from my right hand. Too bad I had to kill him so fast. His powers would've been fun to rip.

"Self-clean," I muttered.

My armor's nanites quickly ate up every bit of foreign matter (blood, dirt, etc.) from my wardrobe in a matter of seconds. I turned off the metalformer's power and shrank to my true size. The nanites figured that the threat was over and receded back into my suit. I enjoyed the chilly faux breeze as I retrieved my guns and spare mags from the dead metalformer.

While I was doing that, Seamus was wisely calling for help on a small hand radio. After all, he had a swarm of mobsters downstairs (some of them supers). They could be a problem. I holstered one of my Glocks. Then I raised the other one and aimed at Seamus' thick skull. I needed to kill this bastard and then get the fuck outta here before –

Both our heads snapped toward the entrance as a flurry of gunshots and muffled explosions broke out downstairs. I almost forgot about my contractors. I was in the shit and they wanted in on the fun. But how'd they know that?

Then I looked around the restaurant and remembered that they had stashed some minicams out here. Part of the extraction plan called for surveillance in every major section of the *Versantio*. My guys hacked into the hotel's security cameras and then planted minicams near any possible points of interest—like this restaurant.

Just like that, the gunfire ceased. My phone rang. I fished it out and answered it with my left hand while my right still aimed the Glock at Seamus' face. The fat man dropped the radio and held his arms up, rightfully afraid for his life.

"Benjamin Cly," I answered with a neutral tone.

"You'd better tip us, boss!" Pinpoint said, her voice flush with triumph.

I approached Seamus, who hadn't moved a muscle and was visibly sweating.

"Status?"

"Stable," she replied. "Most of these idiots left their guns at home. Everyone with powers or hardware went running for the stairs and elevators."

"So what did you do?"

"We blew the elevator cables and shot anyone who took the stairs."

I had to smile.

"What about the folks in the banquet hall?" I asked. "You spread that counteragent yet?"

"It slipped our minds," Pinpoint joked.

"Good," I replied with a glance at my watch. Another twenty minutes and they'd start passing out. "Bug out and lock 'em in the banquet hall. Any casualties?"

"Dodson and Mikura are down," she replied. "Also, half the local PD's headed this way."

"Then get ghost, young lady."

Pinpoint ran into view, a smoking submachine gun in her hands. A Bluetooth was clamped to her right ear. Someone else's blood was splattered across her uniform.

"I plan to," she replied. "Once you take your counteragent."

Ah. Right.

Per the original extraction plan, I had to drug myself. Otherwise, the O'Flernans would suspect that I had something to do with Mockre's extraction. Pinpoint handed me a fat white pill. Everyone on my team had taken one, prior to the op, just in case they had to consume any of the laced beverages. I dry-swallowed the pill as Pinpoint gave the scene an appraising once-over. Then she looked up at me, visibly impressed by my handiwork.

"So . . . they aren't paying us, huh?" Pinpoint asked with fake sadness.

"Look, lad," Seamus said with a genuine tremor in his tone. "This can all be fixed and forgiven. But you have to do the job! If you don't, we're both dead! We're all dead!"

He was telling the truth . . . just not enough of it. I glanced over at Pinpoint and put my gun away.

"Light him up," I ordered without hesitation.

I turned to leave as Pinpoint raised her subgun, eager to kill an honest-to-God mob boss. Couldn't blame her. This was a momentous occasion, of sorts.

"Wait! Please!" Seamus yelled at Pinpoint. Then he shifted his gaze to me as I stopped and turned to face him. "Just listen! If you kill me, there will be all-out war in this town!"

"Or maybe not," I countered. "I'll try to keep a lid on things. None of the other mobs really wants to burn the status quo."

"Think, goddamn you!" Seamus roared, spittle flying from his mouth. "You can't just gun me down and walk away! I run this fucking city!"

The old man just wouldn't admit that his time was up. He had forgotten that Pillar City existed before him. It would exist long after he was gone. I thoughtfully stared at Seamus for a moment and reviewed the pros and cons of letting him live.

Pinpoint curiously awaited my final decision.

So did he.

"Good-bye, Seamus."

I gave Pinpoint the nod. My contractor's gun chattered away on full-auto. When she lowered it, Seamus O'Flernan's corpse lay slumped in its chair, minus his face. Every bullet struck home, from the neck-up. Pinpoint was savoring her kill like a work of art.

Sirens blared in the distance.

"Shall we?" Pinpoint asked as she swapped her weapon's empty mag for a fresh one.

"Let's," I replied and turned away from the remnants of the late Seamus O'Flernan.

CHAPTER FOUR

Pinpoint adjusted her Bluetooth receiver.

"Retrieval! You're up!"

After listening to the reply, she glanced at her watch.

"What's our next move?" Pinpoint asked.

I'd have to talk my way out of this—and fast. Seamus O'Flernan's death left me with one giant mess and a bunch of new enemies. If I screwed this up, my head would be on some killer's trophy wall within a week.

"You have minicams up here?" I asked.

"Three," she replied. "You need them gone?"

"If you would," I smiled.

"Blow the rooftop minicams," Pinpoint ordered and then looked up at me. "You want the footage?"

I nodded, pleased by her efficiency.

"Send the boss a file with all three angles," she ordered. "Full duration."

Seconds later, three tiny explosions went off in the background: one behind Seamus' corpse, the second in the restaurant's kitchen, and the third by the main entrance. That should slow the cops down long enough for me to invent creative ways to steer their investigation toward someone else. With Seamus dead, Pillar City's finest would be chomping at the bit to find his killer and serve up some justice—or risk losing tons of future O'Flernan bribe money.

Retrieval arrived in a gushing implosion of air.

His call sign was "Anywhere" because his teleportation range was planetary. Dressed in a black SWAT-style tactical uniform, the teleporter looked ridiculous. His "costume" was covered with pouches and extra pockets, which he loaded with everything from spare ammo to snack bars. Add on two extra layers of chest armor and Anywhere looked to be in his third trimester.

In his gloved hands was a double-barreled shotgun. Sawed-down to a concealable length, it was an ideal weapon for someone who had the gun skills of a blind snail. Anywhere's black helmet covered the matching balaclava he used to conceal his nerdy, weak-chinned face. At an unremarkable 5'5", 155 pounds, he didn't wear all of that shit to feel like a badass. The kid was simply smart enough to know he was fragile. If he wasn't my best teleporter, I'd have sent him back to MIT with a bottle of steroids and some *Miracle Grow.*

"Someone call for an extraction?" Anywhere grinned.

"My hero!" Pinpoint replied with a cheesy, over-the-top smile.

A stray O'Flernan mobster appeared at the door with a Glock in hand. The well-dressed, mustached Irish mobster saw Seamus' corpse. Then he scowled as he raised his gun. Without even looking his way, Pinpoint sprayed the O'Flernan with a short burst. The poor guy's chest sprouted blood as he crumpled to the ground like corpses do.

"Now where'd he come from?" Pinpoint pondered, her eyes still on me.

My guns half-drawn, I shrugged and then put them back in their holsters. That's when I noticed that Anywhere—amateur that he was—had actually dropped his shotgun. Hands raised in sheer cowardice, he was about to beg the dead guy not to kill him. Pinpoint bit back a giggle as she lowered her weapon. I'd have to get that kid psi-trained before he got himself (or me) killed.

"Pick that up and get me to *The Depravity,*" I muttered.

Pinpoint and Anywhere looked at me like I was nuts. Maybe they were right.

"Should I call in some heavy-hitters?" Pinpoint asked. "After this, you'll need all the backup you can get."

"I'm setting up an impromptu meeting on neutral ground," I explained as Anywhere retrieved his 12-gauge. "You and the others need to get the hell out of town while I try to head off a mob war."

More worried about me than herself, Pinpoint nodded as she turned to regard Seamus' corpse. The poor gal had killed him, knowing that the O'Flernans would hunt her to the ends of the earth for doing so. What made Pinpoint the perfect asset was that she didn't give a fuck. Whatever came next, she'd face it with a smile and a loaded weapon.

Anywhere, however, wasn't enjoying this at all. As he holstered his shotgun, the teleporter finally noticed Seamus and his dead bodyguards. To his credit, the kid didn't puke (this time).

"Does this mean I'm fired?" Pinpoint asked with genuine sadness.

I hadn't expected that question, so I thought on it for a moment.

"Call it a leave of absence," I assured her. "Expect too much money to pop into your account very soon. Once he drops me off, Anywhere's gonna leave you in another time zone. When he does, fall off the grid. Get a new face, hide your gun skills, and wait for my call."

"Where do I take her?" Anywhere asked.

"Your call," I replied. "Just don't tell me where. I might have to give her up."

Anywhere frowned, bothered by the idea of me selling her out.

"Do what you have to do, boss," Pinpoint said, with an indifferent glance at Seamus' corpse. "I can play hide-n-seek with the best of 'em."

I bumped fists with my ace shooter. She stepped back as Anywhere moved up next to me. He didn't have to touch me to teleport us away but being in close-proximity never hurt.

"What about your one o'clock with Grace?" Pinpoint asked.

"This takes precedence," I replied. "Call her and reschedule . . . on your way out of town."

"Good luck," she replied with a solemn, farewell nod.

Then we were gone.

The teleportation made my ears pop as Anywhere put us on the bow of *The Depravity*.

The one-time supertanker had been hollowed out and turned into a floating tribute to all things decadent. The red-and-black ship contained a Vegas-worthy casino, five-star brothel, and plenty of other amenities. Its indoor arena was the main draw, since the games played there were almost always to the death.

"Good enough?" Anywhere asked, eager to get off the ship.

The Depravity's teleportation jammers emitted harmless waves that interfered with his ability. Designed to cut back on teleportation-assisted crimes, it ensured that folks trying to cause mischief on *The Depravity* had no quick exit. The bow was the only gap in the ship's jamming field—a courtesy for high-rolling guests.

"It'll do," I replied.

Anywhere gave me a nervous wave before he vanished with an implosion of air. To my left were the distant lights of the Big Apple. To my right were those of Pillar City's Uptown. *The Depravity* stayed in the span of ocean between the two cities, within easy reach of high-end clients from either metropolis. Most folks were ferried in by boat or helicopter.

My phone beeped. I checked it and found an email with multiple file attachments (each listed with a digital time stamp). I brought up the last one, which included Seamus O'Flernan's last meal. He ate it with his bodyguards standing around him. The busty serving chick came and left throughout his meal, tending to his needs. She must've run off when Seamus' guys rushed me.

The rest of the file had the footage of Seamus' execution and the events leading up to it. I tucked the phone away and ignored the cold air around me.

Harlot, the bitch who ran this floating den of vice, knew I didn't like coming here. She worked for the Wung Triad, a clan of Chinese mobsters who had a strong presence in Pillar City for almost a century. They had global operations and specialized in three areas: gambling, prostitution, and money laundering. If you were in Pillar City, a Wung entertainment spot was never too far away. They were fun, clean, and guarded by no-nonsense bastards with decent aim.

Tonight, this boat was my only hope.

Having sailed these waters for almost twenty years, *The Depravity* had become neutral ground. The authorities and the media pretended that it didn't exist. Even when real super heroes openly flew these skies, they never interfered. Violence wasn't tolerated on the ship unless it involved a sanctioned death match within its arena. It was understood that anyone who even spat on *The Depravity* was in for a gruesome demise.

In my case, it was the perfect meeting ground.

Assuming the Wungs were cool with me hosting a conference on their boat, I'd invite Harlot and a rep from each of the other big mobs: the Povchenkos (Russians), the Vapparez Cartel (Colombians), and the O'Flernans. The nice thing about *The Depravity* was that soldiers from all four mobs should already be here (having illicit fun of some kind) on a Friday night.

The O'Flernans would be tricky to deal with (once word spread of Seamus' demise). Unless I was wrong, Deidre O'Flernan should be the new boss. A twenty-something cokehead with a rep for raging outbursts, she was always jet setting from one party spot to another. Deidre hated her dad more than this town. Worse, the apparent heir to the O'Flernan dynasty lacked her father's wits, people skills, or any experience in the criminal trade. Seamus had spoiled her rotten, hoping that she'd settle down, get married, and push out a few grandsons someday.

It would be a miracle if Deidre took the reins and averted a civil war within the O'Flernan ranks. The mob's operations were definitely worth killing for. Seamus didn't name her—or anyone else—as his successor. If Deidre died or disappeared without a trace, the O'Flernan underbosses could break up the mob or rule it like a board of directors. The last thing I'd expect them to allow was any infighting.

The O'Flernan smuggling empire depended on every port working in sync with the others. Their next boss might have to murder his (or her) way to the top but not through war. Besides, if the Irish didn't stick together, they'd look weak.

Fortunately, the Pillar City mobs co-existed fairly well—both with me and with each other. They'd want to avoid unwanted publicity and preserve their steady profits. The alternative was an expensive conflict between four large mobs with no guarantee of victory or survival.

Keeping the peace should be the easy part. Persuading them not to kill me wouldn't be so simple.

The sooner I showed the footage of Seamus' last minutes, the more likely it would be believed. To those who worked the shady side of the law, my actions were more than justified.

Still, I had much to answer for.

A deck hatch slid open behind me. Underneath was a circular steel platform. I stepped on it. It descended. As soon as my head disappeared below the hatch, the doorway slid closed. The platform descended into the floor of a small, metal-lined room. The doorway in front of me opened on its own.

On the other side stood Harlot.

The vain Chinese bitch aged well. Probably in her mid-40's, she could easily inspire guilty pleasures. The black stiletto heels brought her to 5'7" or so. Her white, low-cut party gown was slit down the left side to reveal her hourglass figure and too much leg. Harlot's buoyant cleavage was fake, as was her whitened smile and that styled mass of black weave on her head. The braided loops in her "hair" were pinned together with a trio of thin, four-inch throwing blades.

Cute.

The makeup was subtler than normal, as was the fragrance she wore tonight. There was a jeweled ring on every finger. A fat blue emerald bracelet was always on her left wrist. Harlot's almond eyes sized me up like a cat with a potential meal in her sights. Because of my status in the local underworld, she greeted me alone. Besides, the bitch didn't need guards. If she wanted to, Harlot could kill me all by herself.

I thought back to eight years ago, when Harlot lost her temper in my general direction. I was meeting with a prospective client who wanted to disappear in a hurry. He was scared and didn't want to mention who was after him. Once he slapped a hundred grand (in Euros) in my hand, I stopped being curious. That's when Harlot crashed the meeting with seven Triad goons at her back. My new client had just scammed her out of ten million Euros, which left her in a vendetta kind of mood.

I gave her my fee and tried to calm things down but she wasn't having it. Harlot angrily suggested that I go somewhere else and kill myself out of guilt for my many sins. Overwhelmed by her psychic influence, I walked off and tried to kill myself—a lot.

While I knew at a glance that she had the power of verbal suggestion, I didn't expect it to be so ridiculously strong. It wasn't like a hypnotic voice, which involved using subliminal waves. No, Harlot was a purebred psychic with a unique form of mental compulsion. Once she hit you with logic (whether you agreed with it or not), your mind was fucked.

Once I was out of the way, Harlot's henchmen retrieved the stolen money and beat the poor idiot to death. Then Harlot carried on with her day . . . and forgot all about me. Hours later, Chu Wung himself heard what Harlot had done. A satisfied customer of mine, the Triad boss angrily told Harlot to clean up her mess.

She eventually found me in Uptown. I had just survived a run-in with an oncoming freight train. By then, I was more than halfway dead. Even with my armor, I had almost killed myself in a hundred-plus different ways. The longer I tried, the more creative— and destructive—I got. Luckily, my armor's nanites reasoned that I needed saving. Thus, when I tried to take the armor off, nothing would unfasten and the armored skin kept protecting me.

Harlot simply suggested that I disregard her earlier suggestion and re-embrace my criminal lifestyle. Seconds later, I was myself again. She was lucky I was too banged up or I would've killed her ass right then and there. Instead, I ended up limping away to the nearest healer.

As Harlot was one of Chu Wung's top people, I couldn't have her killed . . . yet. Still, she correctly guessed that I had a grudge. A day later, Harlot wired two million Euros into my personal account and sent a pair of shapely "nurses" to "check my vitals."

Bitch.

Amazingly, no one else seemed to know about her suggestion power. Folks just thought that she was really persuasive. The only reason Harlot didn't run the Triad was that her power wasn't absolute. Anyone with a strong enough will or implanted psychic defenses (like Chu Wung) could resist her suggestions.

"Mr. Cly," her accented voice purred, "what a pleasant surprise!"

I leaned in close as if to tell her a secret. Harlot read my body language and leaned in as well. My lowered left arm barely touched her right shoulder. During that brief contact, I ripped her power.

"Sorry to arrive unannounced," I said in a low, urgent tone. "But I need a teleconference room—something with a holoprojector."

"I'm sorry but they're all occupied," she replied with a slight shake of her head.

I sighed.

"One million," I flatly stated.

Harlot didn't flinch. Hell, she didn't look impressed at all. The hard truth was that she was an aging, high-level gangster whose sole task was to manage *The Depravity* and keep the profit margins growing. As long as she did this, Harlot's position was safe and loaded with juicy perks. If those profit margins ever dropped too far, she'd end up in an urn like her predecessors. Needless to say, she rarely did anything that would potentially disrupt the Wungs' business interests.

"The next available opening will be Monday morning," Harlot politely explained with pure ice in her tone. "Perhaps you'd like to make a reservation, like everyone else?"

My jaw clenched. Yes, I could use Harlot's own power on her—but only as a last resort. We were being observed through hidden cameras. If she gave in to my request, without ripping me off, it would look suspicious.

"I'll throw in another million when you stuff the seats with the highest-ranking mobsters on this boat. Just from the four mobs—no one else."

Harlot's right eyebrow slightly arched.

Silent moments passed.

"No," she replied. "Those rooms are reserved for high-level negotiations only. The deals at stake are worth far more than a paltry $2 million. I will not offend any of our major clients."

I stepped around and got into her face.

"Do it right-fucking-now and I'll even throw in a third million."

"And if I fucking don't?" Harlot arrogantly whispered back, her lips brushing against my right ear.

She liked money. Clearly, however, she didn't like me. Odds were that the walls around us were loaded with hidden weaponry. Harlot could rain death on me with a word. Or, she could attack me with whatever hidden weapons she had on her. I needed to shake her back into reality without grabbing her by the throat and making her suck my Glock, which was pretty tempting right now.

I backed off with a shrug and kicked on her power.

"Then I'll leave," I said with a fake smile.

Harlot drew back at that unexpected reply.

"And in a few days, when Pillar City's on fire, word'll get out that you could've helped stop it but didn't."

That got her attention. I chuckled as I turned my back to her.

"Once his local profits nosedive, Chu Wung's gonna wonder what else you've been keeping from him. He's gonna have his people pry into your affairs. If Chu Wung doesn't like what he finds, you're dead."

I thoughtfully sauntered a few steps away.

"But don't worry Harlot," I teased. "I'm sure you have nothing to hide. Nothing at all."

Chu Wung loved only one thing more than himself: money. He was notoriously intolerant of anyone whose actions harmed his bottom line (especially his own people). The O'Flernan situation could do exactly that, especially if war broke out. Then there was the matter of Harlot's "dirty little secrets." Anyone in charge of *The Depravity* had to be running shit on the side (things she wouldn't want Wung to know about).

"Wait," she bristled.

I turned around with a satisfied smile and cut off her power. Harlot reluctantly raised the emerald bracelet to her chin.

"Arrange Room 12," she said in Mandarin.

As I approached, she sighed and looked me in the eye.

"Should I expect violence at this impromptu event, Mr. Cly?" Harlot asked in English.

"Don't you always?" I grinned.

Harlot's look of displeasure spoke volumes. Not giving a fuck, I shifted my mind to the negotiations ahead.

"This way," Harlot frowned as she abruptly turned and passed through an open hatchway.

CHAPTER FIVE

Harlot led me toward one of the upper decks and then into a long, narrow corridor. Her heels clacked loudly off the polished, wood-paneled floors. The white plaster walls were lined with murals depicting Chinese landscapes. Each piece was worthy of a museum or a private gallery's main room. Black metal doors were spaced on either side of the hallway, each unmarked and leading into a meeting room. She stopped at the sixth one on the left.

The door was already ajar.

"I hope this location will suffice," Harlot said with a slight, tense bow.

I gave her an imperious nod before I entered.

The rectangular room was white-walled with an ovular mahogany table at its center. Six black rolling chairs were stationed around it. A black, pyramid-shaped holoprojector was built into the center of the table's surface. I caught the strong scent of cigar smoke and realized that Harlot had indeed interrupted someone else's meeting.

I looked down at the floor.

Made up of thick, one-way glass, anyone in here could see the casino's roulette tables (one deck below). If any of the downstairs gamblers were to look up, they'd only see a mirrored ceiling.

"Perfect," I said with a half-turn in her direction.

"Will you need refreshments?" Harlot asked.

"A full spread, please. The higher the alcohol content, the better."

Harlot nodded and stepped out of the room.

I pulled my phone out and dialed Benny Shank, one of my money launderers. While the Wungs laundered most of the dirty money in this town, I didn't trust them with mine. I had a few independent "financiers" on my payroll—just for times like these. I told Benny to cut up three million and wire the payments to a few dozen of Chu Wung's corporate fronts within the hour.

The second I hung up, a trio of Chinese serving ladies entered. Pretty enough to double as runway models, they wore black silk gowns adorned with golden-colored floral print. They pushed in three carts, which were loaded with snacks and booze. Without a word, the ladies picked a corner and stood there, ready to serve upon request.

Thinking of Pinpoint's server disguise, I wondered if they were part of *The Depravity's* security detail. I couldn't see any super powers on them. Still, they could be packing all kinds of weapons and/or combat implants under those loose-fitting gowns. I politely declined any refreshments and waited for the reps to arrive.

Minutes later, Harlan Ronns entered the room.

In his early fifties, the O'Flernan mobster had a graying brown buzz cut and an air of casual menace. Ronns strode up in brown cotton slacks and a black dress shirt. He finished a bottle of micro-brewed beer and dropped it into a nearby metal trash can. Ronns then noticed me as he slung his brown suit jacket over his right shoulder. His face twisted with recognition and curiosity . . . but not anger. That was surprising because he should've been notified of Seamus' death by now.

The O'Flernan underbosses were assigned to different port cities and ran them like criminal franchises. Most of their profits flowed to Seamus who (until recently) oversaw Pillar City's operations. Every O'Flernan underboss was assigned a Shepherd: someone responsible for coordinating security for that particular port zone. Seamus picked the term "Shepherd" because of its biblical connotation. An O'Flernan Shepherd would protect his criminal "flock" and inflict Old

Testament-style retribution upon any and all of their enemies.

Not just anyone could be a Shepherd. Only loyal, skilled, veteran sadists were even considered for that bloody mantle. To keep them from getting too ambitious, it was made clear that Shepherds could never become underbosses. Still, it was considered a position of honor within the family.

Harlan Ronns was Pillar City's Shepherd.

Before tonight, we got along well enough. If anyone asked, I would've described him as an overqualified street soldier who seemed to be satisfied with his role. Knowing Ronns' vicious sense of loyalty, Seamus' murder would make us mortal enemies within the hour.

Sleeves rolled up, Ronns exposed a pair of strong, tattooed arms. His handsome, tanned face showed both intelligence and mocking aggression as he stepped over to the serving girls and gave them a leering once-over. They gave him their fake smiles of shy subservience while he grabbed a fresh bottle of beer and a clump of green grapes.

Then he looked my way as he sat at the opposite end of the table.

"Hello, Cly," he greeted with a slightly rural accent.

"Ronns," I replied with a nod.

Not all Irish mobsters came from Ireland or some East Coast city. Even though Ronns was from Ohio, his ethnic pedigree was real enough.

"You the reason I was pulled off a really soft blonde just now?"

"Afraid so," I apologetically shrugged.

Ronns sized me up as he took a deep swig and then set his beer down.

"You look like a man in trouble, Mr. Cly. This about that Mockre matter?"

"Partially."

"Heh!" Ronns chuckled. "Wish I could've been there. But the old man gave me the night off."

As the city's Shepherd, Ronns should've been the one who cut out Mockre's tongue. He also should've died on that rooftop, along with Seamus and his bodyguards. Instead, he was drinking and whoring on *The Depravity*.

"So, what's this about?"

"Something messy," I replied. "I want the others here before I show this footage."

Ronns shrugged and glanced at his gold Rolex. Then he sat down, ate grapes, and patiently watched the gambling below.

Five minutes later, Carlos Eduardo Nunez entered the room.

The short, chubby Latino was in his late 50's. His thinning hair was dyed black. Worry lines were all but seared into his face. Nunez sported a platinum wedding band on his left hand. He wore a conservative white suit with a pair of pink panties peeking out of the left trouser pocket. There was also a small drink stain on his sky-blue polo-style shirt.

While I believed that Nunez wasn't Colombian, he worked for them. More of a senior accountant than an underboss or enforcer, he was still high enough on the food chain to be at this table. The Vapparez Cartel ran a "pharmaceutical monopoly" in Pillar City. Any narcotics of value—from weed to power augmentation serums—were solely supplied by them.

For a glorified paymaster, Nunez was an okay sort of criminal. He crunched numbers in an honest way and monitored the cartel's legitimate investments. Whenever the Colombians paid a bill, bribe, or whatever, Nunez signed their checks. Not knowing what was going on here, he looked a bit worried as he picked a chair to Ronns' left.

"Sorry to interrupt your . . . other meeting," I grinned.

"Bah!" Nunez scoffed with a mild accent as he sat down. "I could use the break. Viagra's not kicking in as fast as I'd like."

Ronns almost choked on his beer as he suppressed his laughter. Nunez was too tipsy to care as he pointed at a bottle of champagne. One of the serving gals took the hint and poured him a glass.

"So, what's this about?" Nunez asked as he leaned back into his chair.

"Cly has a little 'show-n-tell' for us," Ronns said before he wiped some beer from his chin.

"Ah," Nunez replied as he accepted his champagne with a grateful nod.

While Ronns was a mere human, Nunez was a low-end super. His only power was a perfect memory. The guy could recall every moment of his life, down to what it felt like to be born. Or every transaction he ever laid eyes upon.

I suspected that the Colombians gave him psychic defenses—probably an artificial psi-shield of some kind. The bean-sized devices were typically implanted within the brain and were much cheaper than the psi-screens in Mockre's head.

Psi-shields jammed the flow of psychic energy, which blocked most forms of telepathy or mind control. The cartel also liked psi-shields because they could be accessorized. I've seen implants that came with tracking beacons, audio-visual bugs, suicide devices, and other nasty features—all designed to keep the wearer from giving up vital information.

As Nunez took his first sip of champagne, Harlot re-entered the room with Piotor Spetrovich of the

Povchenko mob. Of all the Russian mob "captains" in the area, Harlot had to find the king dick of the bunch. In the arms trade, Spetrovich was a thirtysomething "man diva" with an elite skill set and no tact. Black-haired, beak-nosed, and sharp-chinned, you could take just one look at his beady little blue eyes and know that he was an asshole.

Tall and skinny, the pasty-faced weapons geek was arguably one of the most dangerous minds on the planet. On par with The Outfitter, Spetrovich could design any weapon imaginable . . . and a few that weren't. But I couldn't read any powers in him. That meant his abilities were either masked (like mine) or tech-based.

Spetrovich wore black denim jeans, a red t-shirt (with the old Soviet flag), and a black leather jacket. The gray-and-brown cowboy boots were tasteless but were (most likely) carved off a real animal of some kind.

Then there was his utility belt—a gaudy symbol of what made him dangerous.

It was fashioned out of a bright, white leather with over a dozen pouches. If the stories were true, the belt was Spetrovich's private arsenal. Guns and knives were tolerated on *The Depravity.* The stuff in his belt, however, could probably sink the ship. Harlot cut Spetrovich some slack only because the Russian had spent so much money over the years.

Spetrovich moved behind Ronns, who subtly shifted his grip on the beer bottle—like he wanted to swat the Russian with it. The asshole didn't say a word as he strolled past the three Chinese ladies and surveyed the snacks at hand. He grabbed a bottle of vodka and a bunch of cheese blocks with his left hand. Dumping them onto a gold saucer, he finally plopped down across from Nunez.

Unlike Ronns or Nunez, Spetrovich came here for the fights. He got off on watching people die. For a

moment, I wondered if he knew about Seamus. Then he
looked over at the holoprojector with a sudden, tobacco-
stained smile. He knew.

"You fucking filmed it?!" Spetrovich chuckled as
he eyed the device, his accent annoyingly thick.

I nodded.

"Oh Ronns!" The Russian raved. "You're in for
some fun tonight!"

The others gave me curious looks as Harlot
gestured for her serving wenches to leave. They did,
closing the door on the way out.

"The floor is yours, Mr. Cly," Harlot said with a
polite smile.

With a sigh, I pulled out my phone.

"You're dead!" Ronns jumped to his feet.
"Whatever it costs! Wherever you run! YOU. ARE.
DEAD. MOTHERFUCKER!!"

The red-faced Irishman glared at me through the
holoimage of Seamus O'Flernan's corpse. The minicam
file had been uploaded into the holoprojector, which
showed the gruesome footage in 3D perfection.

Ronns' right hand darted into his suit jacket. I
figured that it had been designed to conceal any number
of weapons. Before he could pull something out, Harlot
quickly stepped up and whispered something into his left
ear. Her mere words (whatever they were) held Ronns at
bay. What impressed me was that she talked him down
without her power. I suppressed a smile and looked
around.

Nunez leaned back into his chair, looking way more
sober. Most likely, his mind was racing over the
implications (good and bad) of Seamus' death. My
actions had thrown this town's criminal equation into a

whole new direction. The tension on his face seemed to indicate that he didn't foresee a happy outcome.

Spetrovich looked disappointed that Ronns hadn't shot me yet. Then his eyes strayed to my suit with piqued interest. Based on the footage, he saw that it was more than met the eye. For him to be interested in my armor was a bit fucking scary.

Harlot looked worried. After all, she disliked big changes to the status quo. For years, the four mobs co-existed in relative harmony. Hell, they even (exclusively) used each other's services. The Irish shipped contraband for the other three mobs. The Colombians supplied the drugs. The Russians sold them killing appliances. While the other mobs didn't trust the Chinese with their money laundering, they did party/whore/gamble at their parlors.

Rather than fight over territory, Pillar City's abundant domain was shared. Only criminal fronts and legitimate businesses were exclusively held by any one mob. What kept the arrangement stable was that each outfit stayed within its own lucrative specialty. It was a good idea (one thought up by Seamus himself in the early 70's).

The old man's death would definitely rock the status quo. If the O'Flernan mob fell apart or stopped shipping their wares, the other mobs could lose billions.

"After you killed him, why didn't you run?" Nunez asked. "With your resources, you might've made it."

"There wasn't a need to run," I sincerely replied. "The simple truth was that he had it coming."

Harlot preemptively touched Ronns' right shoulder. The Irishman scowled at her for a moment. Then he nodded her away, but his right hand still hovered near his jacket's hidden arsenal. Harlot sat down at the table as well, curious as to what my solution was.

"Think about it," I explained. "Mockre was a traitor. The O'Flernans paid me a half-million to go over his bona fides. We find out he was spying on his own people. He got killed. That was supposed to be that."

"Why were you there?" Harlot asked.

"I was invited," I replied. "And I brought my contractors in for two reasons. One, if the feds busted in—and things went sideways—my people would get me out. The second reason was Mockre himself."

"What do you mean?" Spetrovich asked as he munched on some cheese.

"We couldn't prove that he was a fed but his surveillance equipment was government-issue."

"Who did he work for, anyway?" Nunez asked Ronns.

"No idea," Ronns admitted.

"We kept digging for that answer, up until the last possible moment," I explained.

"If we had learned that Mockre was a black ops asset, we'd have pulled him."

"Why?" Nunez asked.

"Killing a super spy's bad for business," Ronns grudgingly acknowledged. "I told Seamus as much, but he wouldn't listen."

"Our plan was for a non-lethal extraction," I continued. "We'd only move in if we could figure out his real loyalties in time. But Mockre had some wicked psi-screening. Unsure of where the fucker came from, I gave the order to let the O'Flernans finish him off."

"Just like that?" Spetrovich teased. "You're cold, Cly."

I glared at Spetrovich like he was a spider in need of a good stomping.

"Then Seamus figured he'd set me up," I continued.

That changed the mood. They knew I was right but none of them wanted to admit it.

"How do you know the offer wasn't legit?" Nunez asked.

Spetrovich mockingly giggled through a mouthful of cheese.

"You don't get out much, do you?! It's a power grab."

"How do you mean?" Ronns asked.

Spetrovich leaned back into his chair, folded his hands behind his head, and sighed.

"If you were Cly and I was Seamus, I'd hire you for a bogus job. You take my money and send your best people. Then I'd kill you and blame a fictional outfit, like The Black Wheel. No one suspects me because I paid you so much goddamned money. After your funeral, I'd quietly hire your contractors. Or even better, have an outside fixer take your place. And no one's the wiser."

The asshole had a point.

"Whether you like him or not, Cly's contractors are the best," Spetrovich continued. "If Seamus' 'proxy fixer' took over Cly's operations and earned that same level of confidence, he could've spied on all of us with ease."

"Or take us out, one-by-one," Nunez reasoned.

Spetrovich nodded in agreement. We all looked over at Ronns. The Shepherd didn't answer. He merely shook his head in stubborn denial. Ronns didn't want to admit that Seamus loved his devious little schemes. Taking over my firm wouldn't have been out of the question.

Still, why would the old smuggler want my firm? He had plenty of muscle throughout the world, with plenty of Shepherds to guide them. If his people had a tricky job, they outsourced to fixers like me. Seamus didn't need the headaches involved with being a fixer.

It just didn't track.

"Right now, we've only got theories," I admitted. "It's possible that there really is a Black Wheel out there and that Seamus was afraid for his life. After all, he did offer me way more money than the job was worth. That's when I realized the offer wasn't legit. When I turned him down, shit got ugly."

"You could've just walked away," Harlot argued.

"I was about to," I stiffly reminded her, "Right before three supers tried to kill me."

The room went silent.

"Has anyone ever heard of them?" Harlot asked the others. "This 'Black Wheel' group?"

"No," Nunez replied.

Ronns shook his head.

"An urban legend," Spetrovich confidently lied. "A bunch of bored, aging super villains is the rumor."

I looked over at Harlot. She didn't believe him either.

"Who's that woman?" Nunez asked Ronns. "The chesty one with the skirt?"

"No idea," Ronns replied.

I grabbed the holoprojector's remote and rewound the footage. Somewhere before the fight, Seamus' female server just stepped off-camera and disappeared.

"A fourth bodyguard?" I asked.

"No," Harlot shook her head. "A bodyguard would've gotten Seamus out of there during the fight. Instead, she left him behind to die."

"None of them are O'Flernan," Ronns said with cold certainty. More intrigued than angry, he pulled his hand out of the suit jacket. "The old man would never let outsiders protect him."

He looked my way.

"None of his normal people were around?" Ronns asked.

"Not when I got there."

"Maybe he was afraid there was another mole," Spetrovich chimed in.

Ronns pulled out his phone and turned it on, which explained why he hadn't heard about Seamus' death earlier. He started to text something.

"Let's talk about your trigger-happy girlfriend," Spetrovich smiled.

My face hardened as I thought of Pinpoint. I was actually starting to hope that she'd slip through the cracks.

"She acted on my order," I replied.

"Tell that to the 47 dead Irish mobsters left at the *Versantio*," the Russian chuckled.

Pinpoint didn't mention that part.

"What?!" Ronns looked up from his phone.

I let my sincere surprise show while Nunez and Harlot swapped worried glances.

"That's the word on the Darknet," Spetrovich shrugged, "Of course, your people could've killed everyone else in the room too, right?"

I looked over at Ronns. The Shepherd stared back. Oh yeah—we were mortal enemies. Ronns finished his text and put the phone away.

"So, 'fixer,' what's your solution?" Spetrovich asked.

I took a deep, calming breath.

"Deidre O'Flernan gets kidnapped," I suggested.

Spetrovich and Ronns mockingly laughed. Nunez looked up at the ceiling, kicking the idea's tires. Harlot stood up, paced over to a tray of drinks, and poured herself a flute of white wine.

"This kidnapping will be staged?" Harlot asked in mid-pour.

"It has its benefits," I nodded, relieved that someone was keeping up with me. "Deidre's taken off the streets and put somewhere safe. Play the media right and they'll drum up public sympathy."

"And they'd give a damn because?" Spetrovich asked.

"Because you'll fucking tell them to," I shot back.

It was common knowledge that the mobs had their hooks into the local media for decades. Through a bouquet of bribery, blackmail, and outright threats, they forced the "free" press to drop any stories involving them. Should a reporter or broadcaster ignore this reality, he/she ended up missing soon after.

"Deidre's the heir to the O'Flernan mob," I continued. "But if you let her 'mourn' on her own, she might OD on coke by Monday."

Ronns took a slow, thoughtful sip from his beer.

"Make her an 'innocent victim' and you might keep your political contacts," I bluntly added.

"He's got a point," Nunez said to Ronns. "Without those, you're dead in the water."

"We'd all be fucked!" Ronns snapped with an irritated glance at Nunez. Then his eyes darted back to me.

"And who'd we blame for this fake kidnapping? Hmm? You?"

"Pinpoint," I replied.

The room went thoughtfully quiet. Only Nunez looked disgusted that I'd offer one of my people up so quickly.

"She did pull the trigger," Harlot mused. "As for Deidre, when does she get 'miraculously' rescued?"

"After she's been psi-trained," I smiled.

"Oh you slick fucker!" Spetrovich pounded the table with both fists. "You want to make the bitch competent!"

Ronns glared at the Russian.

I shrugged, surprised that Seamus hadn't done it by now. All it took were a few good telepaths, some skilled mobsters, and one spoiled little mob princess. The telepaths would gather up a copy of the skills, experience, and mindset of Seamus' best mobsters. They'd then pour all that knowledge into Deidre's mind. Along the way, they could purge both her addictions and personality flaws. Frankly, Deidre O'Flernan could be turned into a competent mob boss inside of a few hours.

"And the people you killed?" Ronns asked.

"I can set up a trust fund for their next-of-kin," I offered. "I'm sure the O'Flernans can think of an appropriately painful amount."

I paused for other questions or comments. There weren't any.

"And that's that," I sighed.

Nunez was nervous. Ronns was vengeful. Spetrovich was enjoying this way too much. And Harlot's poker face was in overdrive. She tactfully cleared her throat.

"Thank you for this most intriguing presentation," Harlot said with her best hostess smile. "We will confer with our respective superiors and render a verdict within the hour. Mr. Cly, please wait here—as a gesture of good faith."

Those last words had a special emphasis. My guess was that Harlot had tried to use her suggestion power on me. I nodded, playing along. With that, the jury of my criminal peers left the room to deliberate.

They wouldn't argue over whether or not I was guilty.

They'd only discuss how severe my punishment would be.

CHAPTER SIX

I suppose the meeting could've been worse.

The funny thing was that I had unwittingly given the fuckers new reasons to kill me.

There was Spetrovich, who pointed out the brilliant idea of killing me and taking over my outfit. While I didn't want to admit it, he had a point. I was so busy running my little empire that I never pondered what would happen to it after I died.

Fixers came and went like the seasons.

When a fixer died, his/her organization typically broke apart soon after. Most organizations—legal or illegal—had varying levels of management. Fixers had to run it all or get backstabbed by their subordinates. Thanks to ultramodern tech, I could run my multi-billion-dollar business out of a bathroom stall.

I was the only one with direct access to my client list, mission records, and account files. All of my clients (large and small) directly contacted me. All 412 contractors were paid via untraceable wire transfers that (usually) came from my server. That server was built into the last place anyone would think to look for it—my suit.

Once I fed a job's details into my system, it would select the best available contractors. I double-checked the server's picks, e-mailed the client about the price, and made the necessary arrangements. What bothered me now was that, with a few tweaks, my firm could practically run itself. I had failsafes against someone stealing my business while I was alive . . . but not if I was dead.

Then again, the mobs might kill me because I was too dangerous for my own good. After all, my eight-person extraction team did manage to slaughter almost fifty Irish mobsters—some supers—with only two casualties. Killing Seamus and coming here to parlay meant that I didn't fear them like I should've. They might forget my years of neutral, efficient service and fear that I was out to take over their operations.

Then there were the O'Flernans, who'd come at me until my dying day. That's just vengeful Irish DNA right there. Besides, whoever wanted to unify the different O'Flernan franchises would have an easier time of it by killing me. That accomplishment would cement the next leader's bona fides.

I ignored my need for a drink and a cheap woman. Instead, I pulled out my smokes, watched the roulette tables, and wondered if they'd try to kill me right here and now. The hour slowly passed.

Nunez came in first, looking tired and bothered. He headed for a bottle of whiskey and poured himself a double without looking my way. Ronns walked in with a smug grin on his face. He plopped into his seat and eyed me like a genie had granted him his fondest wish. Spetrovich was toying with a gray device that vaguely resembled a tiny pocket calculator. The weapons geek didn't give me a glance as he sat back down.

Harlot came in last, without her serving gals. One look at her expression and I was concerned. This was a woman who had seen more blood spilled than anyone else in this room. We clearly disliked each other. If Harlot had been brutally killed, I'd have quietly celebrated. Yet, at this moment, I saw genuine pity in her eyes.

Not good.

"You have three choices, Mr. Cly," Harlot announced as she closed the door behind her.

"I'm listening," I replied, a fresh cigarette in my mouth.

"Option A: you leave town right now. If you ever return, you'll be killed."

Harlot said that last part with a cold certainty.

"Would I owe the O'Flernans restitution?" I asked with a thoughtful nod at the Shepherd.

They looked over at Ronns, who shook his head.

"We'll take care of our own, fixer," Ronns replied, talking down to me like I was a two-legged roach.

"Just pack up and take my operations with me, eh?" I asked Harlot.

"Something like that."

I bit back a sarcastic reply.

The look on Harlot's face suggested that this was the option she'd have chosen had she been in my shoes. She must've forgotten what happens to crooks who get kicked out of town. I should know because I was usually hired to have them killed.

First, they got shown the proverbial door and left Pillar City. Yeah, they usually hid in some clever way. Most bought new identities and maybe even changed their faces. They looked over their shoulders for the first year or so. Eventually, they'd let their guard down and start enjoying their new lives. That's when my contractors would come along and kill them with relative ease.

No thanks. I didn't feel like getting shot in the head while perusing the morning paper (possibly by one of my own contractors).

"The other options?" I asked.

"Option B: we take you down to the arena," came her replied. "You have a Death League match against Kristos. Without your suit."

I smiled at Harlot's words, waiting for the punch line. She wasn't joking. Maybe some of them wanted to see if I had super powers or if I had really killed Seamus' bodyguards with just my armor.

"If I win?"

Ronns laughed.

The others looked at me like I was nuts.

I don't think they had even discussed that possibility.

The Death League was an underground street fighting circuit that regularly held matches in *The Depravity's* arena. An independent outfit, they shared a portion of their profits with the Triad. Their membership was exclusively made up of supers, who held highly entertaining fights to the death. Each fighter was an elite, super-powered badass. The lowest of them could kill a champion-level MMA fighter within seconds.

Worse, the Death League's long-reigning champion was a guy named Kristos. Whether that was his real name or just a scary moniker wasn't relevant. What did matter was that whenever Kristos won a match—which was always—he ate his opponent. The cannibal would rip out his foe's organs and feast, right then and there, before the cheering crowds. Most powers couldn't hurt or even slow him down. Could I kill him with no armor and only two ripped powers?

Maybe.

"If you won, that would be the end of it," Harlot lied. "The other mobs will leave you alone."

Ronns smirked at that notion as he met my gaze. Right. The O'Flernans would still come after me. Option B was like Option A—only with a quicker death.

"Option C?" I softly asked.

Harlot started to speak –

"We take it all," Ronns rudely cut in. "Your money. Your contacts. Everything in your name becomes ours."

Spetrovich finished pecking away with a triumphant squeak of delight. Then he put his toy away and expectantly regarded my armor.

"If those are my options, then I'll go with –"

"There's more," Ronns interrupted. "You can leave town. But if you do, you can expect more money on your head than Saddam had when he was sighted in Tehran. Or, you can stay. But if you do, Cly, you have to pay up for that privilege."

"I'm listening."

Ronns leaned forward, eager to nail me with the worst part.

"Community Service."

Only a lifetime of hard discipline kept me from painting the walls with his fucking brains. Another one of Seamus O'Flernan's bright ideas, Community Service was the mob's preference to outright murder. They considered it a mercy usually reserved for someone whose murder could create friction. In this town, fortunes rose and fell all the time. But Community Service called for me to become the lowest of the low— a crime fighter.

Until the 2011 *Clean Sweep*, there were still openly-heroic types patrolling the streets and fighting crime. The public hated them because the crook-owned media told them to. Governments (the world over) hated the heroes because they couldn't control them. Then there was the worst thing about being a hero: the statistically short life span. Most of them didn't last more than two years.

"As long as you are within city limits," Ronns continued, "you cannot be a fixer or any other kind of criminal. You must obey the law. And every night, you have to fight crime."

"Me? A crime fighter?" I quietly asked through clenched jaws.

"Yeah," Spetrovich jovially replied. "Your gut would look great in skintight spandex. Maybe throw in a cape?"

"For how long?" I asked.

"Life," Ronns replied with bitter emphasis.

The longest I ever heard of anyone surviving Community Service was six weeks.

"As is custom," Harlot cut in, "your activities will be closely monitored and even tolerated . . . provided they don't intentionally interfere with organized crime in this city."

"Does this boat count as city limits?" I asked.

Everyone looked at Harlot, who had the final say on who could/couldn't hang out on *The Depravity*.

"It does," she nodded.

"Just shoot yourself, amigo," Nunez slurred. "It's fucking more dignified. There's no money in crime fighting."

Maybe. Maybe not. I thoughtfully exhaled some smoke through my mouth and leaned back into my chair.

"Let me get this straight," I ventured. "You take my money, my business, and my freedom to be a criminal. In exchange, I have to protect the innocent, punish the guilty, and do so without going after your respective mobs. But any other crooks are fair game?"

"Basically," Harlot replied. "As long as you adhere to those terms, you would be safer than you are now. None of us can harm, hinder, or rob you."

"Really?" I half-grinned at Ronns. "So, if a group of mobsters attacked me, unprovoked of course, I could kill them in self-defense?"

Her almond eyes turned toward Ronns and thoughtfully narrowed. The Shepherd scowled back.

"Yes," Harlot truthfully replied. "In fact, you would be avenged if any member of the local mobs was to harm you—at least, while you're abiding by the terms of your service."

That almost sounded fair. Too bad she left out the part where Community Service status wouldn't protect me from anyone who was *unaffiliated* with one of the four mobs. Any indie killer could hunt me down without consequence. With a glance at Ronns, I knew that I'd have a bunch of untraceable, freelance bounties on my head by sunrise.

"Are there any limitations on who can work with me?"

"You can work with anyone you want," Harlot nodded.

"But they're fair game," Ronns grinned, assuming that I'd go running to my contractors for help. "Also, if you have them mess with us, the deal's off and you're dead."

I looked over at Spetrovich, whose eyes were still impatiently locked on my suit . . . like he was waiting for something to happen.

"Okay, asshole," I sighed at the Russian, "What did you do to my armor?"

"Nothing," Spetrovich lied with a dramatic roll of his eyes. "Not that you'll be keeping it, anyway."

Nunez checked his watch with a triumphant chuckle.

"He hacked your armor," Nunez revealed. "Then he bet me five grand that you would try some shit by now."

"And if I had?"

Nunez gave me a sly grin.

"Your armor's self-cleaning nanites would've eaten you like piranhas. And I'd be five grand poorer."

I laughed at Spetrovich as I slipped the cigarette back into my mouth.

"Bullshit! He's too stupid to hack my armor!" I mocked, fairly certain about what would happen next.

Spetrovich shrugged and tapped his device.

One moment, I had an armor suit. The next, it had turned into gray nanodust and fell off me. All I wore now were my black socks, designer blue briefs, my holstered Glocks, and my watch. The contents of my pockets clattered to the floor: wallet, bomb keys, money clip (with eight grand), Marlboros, spare mags, lighter, Smartphone, silver pen, notepad, and a pocket blade.

"Nice abs, Cly!" Spetrovich taunted. "Guess your armor wasn't all that, eh?"

As the Russian weasel laughed and pointed at my exposed belly, I leaned back into my chair and thought of the implications. A crime fighter, eh? With the right angle, I could turn this to my advantage. I might even prosper. Still, it wouldn't be easy.

Nunez cleared his throat and held out his left hand.

Spetrovich eyed the money launderer with open contempt as he pulled a fat wad of cash from his left pocket. He counted out five grand and slapped it on the table. Nunez reached out and took it. After a quick count, the bean counter slid his winnings into his suit jacket, finished his drink, and poured another.

"I'll go with Community Service," I declared, really wanting a bottle for myself.

Only Harlot didn't look surprised.

"There are a number of ongoing jobs which need to be resolved," I added. "May I finish them?"

"No," Harlot softly replied. "As of right now, you belong to the streets, Mr. Cly. As of now . . . you are Pillar City's newest, and only, super hero."

The way she said that was so dramatic that I figured she was "using" her damned power again. I nodded with a resigned sigh.

"Harlot?" I asked evenly, cigarette still in hand.

"Yes, Mr. Cly?"

"Could you have someone bring me something warm to wear?" I glared at Spetrovich, who picked up my money clip and pocketed it with a sneer.

"Certainly," Harlot replied. "A week's worth of clothing is the least we can do after your generous fee for tonight's services."

For the Colombians, Russians, and Chinese, this wasn't personal. They fucked me over because they had to. Ronns probably made all the right threats. Something like if they didn't go along with this penalty, the O'Flernans would stop shipping their contraband. Or worse, the Irish could also sic their political/law enforcement connections on them.

The silver lining was that I could stay in Pillar City, where I knew how everything worked. I could even do business with the other mobs—as long as it was legal.

"Do you need my financials?" I asked with a forced smile.

"No need," Ronns grinned. "Your liquid accounts shouldn't be a problem to seize. We'll have it all in a few hours."

Surprised, I looked over at Spetrovich who innocently shrugged and looked over his gray device. Apparently, he was disappointed by what he saw.

"It was clever of you to hide your server within your armor's nanocode," he admitted. "Who designed it?"

"An old friend," I cryptically replied.

I thought of Samir and what he'd do when he found out that his custom-made suit had been destroyed by a Russian gadget-bitch.

"What about non-cash assets?" I asked. "With my files deleted, they might be hard to find."

Over the years, some of my clients paid me in everything from cash to shares of stock to fine art to real estate.

"My stuff's scattered all the world," I explained. "The only inventory list was in my server."

"Whatever we find, we'll take," Nunez shrugged. "We'll give you the transfer paperwork to sign by next Sunday."

I sighed at the thought of them taking my building.

"I'll need a place to stay," I admitted.

"*The Depravity* has suitable cabins," Harlot offered. "You may stay until the paperwork is signed: on the house, of course."

I nodded my gratitude and resumed smoking. I could see the same question on their faces. What was I worth? A few billion, I guess. And they were in for a nasty treat when they split those assets four ways. Not everything in my name was actually mine. To some of my clients, I was like an evil hen that sat on their money-laundered "eggs"—some of which belonged to very dangerous people. When the money went missing, I wonder whom they'd blame for their losses—me or the mobs.

"When do I need to start fighting crime?" I asked.

The mob reps swapped glances.

"Tomorrow night should suffice," Nunez generously offered. "Objections?"

"Nah," Ronns said, bothered that I was taking this turn of events so well.

"More time to gloat," Spetrovich taunted. "We know you're nothing without the armor."

If he only knew. I looked down at the remnants of my beloved suit.

"By the way, Mr. Spetrovich, can you undo that?" I asked with an even tone.

"Undo what?"

"The armor-to-dust thing? Can you undo that?"

"No," Spetrovich sneered. "Your armor's designed to self-destruct if its specs or memory logs were ever in danger of being downloaded. The best I could do was hack your account data."

Damn! I hid my amazement and looked up at the ceiling. Well, as shitty as they were, the terms of my Community Service were set.

I gave him a regretful sigh.

"That's a shame, Mr. Spetrovich," I replied, as my eyes roamed toward the Triad hostess.

"Why?" Spetrovich asked.

"Do you remember the exact moment Harlot declared the start of my Community Service?"

"Yeah," frowned the Russian. "So?"

"Prior to that moment, you destroyed *my* armor."

The room went dead-quiet as the implications set in.

"Doesn't matter," Ronns stubbornly countered. "The armor—what's left of it—is ours now."

"True," I admitted. "But when I spent $3 million renting this conference room, I did so on *The Depravity*. And the Triad has strict rules regarding the destruction of property belonging to a paying customer. When you destroyed it, the armor technically still belonged to me."

Harlot frowned at Spetrovich. Had he only waited twenty seconds longer . . .

"If I wanted to, Mr. Spetrovich, I could have you killed right now."

The Russian looked me in the eye and saw that I was relishing the thought. Spetrovich gave Harlot a nervous glance.

"Mr. Cly has a point," she admitted.

"You dumb shit!" Ronns shouted at Spetrovich. "You're not supposed to fuck with him if he's behaving himself!"

Ronns hated me, but he was old school. Rules were still rules. Violate the rules of the game and the game breaks down. Spetrovich saw the grin on Nunez's drunken face and realized that he had no allies. He had to know that the Wung Triad killed rule breakers over much, much less.

I took a drag from my cigarette.

"Of course, I'm open to fair market compensation," I offered.

"Fine," Spetrovich scowled. "What's your armor worth?"

"$250 million."

Jaws dropped.

"Bullshit!" Spetrovich yelled, before slipping into a tirade of fluent Russian insults about my mother's sexual preferences. I pretended not to understand him. With my left hand, I flicked cigarette ashes over the remnants of my armor.

"How do I know that the armor's worth even half that?!" Spetrovich yelled in English.

With my smoking hand, I shrugged and pointed to the Russian, while giving Harlot a nod.

"He's got a point," I admitted, with an inspired smile. "That's why I got my armor insured in '04. Lloyd's of London charges me an arm-and-a-leg, of course. But they appraised the armor and will vouch for its value."

Nunez almost choked on his drink as he broke into a fit of laughter.

"You had your armor insured?!" Nunez balked.

"Of course," I purred. "Wouldn't you?"

"Isn't his insurance policy an asset?" Ronns asked.

Nunez shook his head.

"More of a hefty expense—until it pays out. And we can't touch a dime of it."

"Why the hell not?!" Ronns groaned.

"Because we can only take his current assets," Nunez patiently explained. "From this moment on, anything Cly earns is his. We can't rob him. Remember?"

As I leaned over and picked up my wallet, I noticed Harlot's grin. She was impressed by the way I baited Spetrovich into hacking my suit. Had I just handed it over, he might've taken it to a lab and figured out a way to pick the server clean without triggering its auto-destruct feature.

Aside from the money trails, my clients' secrets were safe.

I calmly pulled out my insurance card and flicked it toward Harlot.

"I'd also appreciate it if the casino could supply me with an encrypted, secured account with your esteemed EDR package."

That raised eyebrows.

EDR stood for Executive Defense and Retaliation. It was a nifty, barely legal, account feature. When I was a fixer, I couldn't trust the Wungs with my finances. They'd be able to track my transactions, which threatened the privacy of my clients. But as a crime fighter, the EDR was the only feasible way to safely store my new wealth. Besides, laundering my money (into hundreds of smaller accounts) went against the new rules.

Better still, all EDR accounts were insured in their entirety—whether an account's worth $100 or $100 billion. Even law enforcement agencies couldn't freeze my account assets. If I stuffed my money into a regular bank, my account(s) could be stolen or frozen in any number of ways. Hell, Spetrovich could arrange either misfortune within an hour (tops).

But anyone stealing from the EDR endured the wrath of the Wung Triad. It was their pride and joy. To lose a dollar of it would make them lose face: along with billions of dollars worth of current and future business. It's never been robbed. Even the maddest of mad geniuses left the EDR alone.

"We'll have to charge you a 10% service fee," Harlot cautioned. "And you'd need a minimum deposit of $1 million."

I glanced over at Spetrovich.

"Get me my money in the next hour and you'll only owe me $240 million. Deal?"

Spetrovich glared daggers at me . . . then nodded.

"Good," I replied with a satisfied smile.

The door opened and a serving gal showed up with a red suitcase. She set it on the table, in front of me. Then she flipped it open and stepped back. I admired the array of casual, semi-casual, and formal attire. They even threw in a toiletry kit. I grabbed a pair of blue jeans. Pleased that they fit my large ass, I stood up.

"Now, if you'll excuse me," I grinned, "I need to celebrate my career change."

I reached for a black leather belt and began to loop it through my jeans.

"Do you have the required funds, Mr. Spetrovich?" Harlot asked with a threatening frown.

She didn't care about his status on the Russian mob's food chain. If Spetrovich broke the rules on her boat, his life was forfeit.

"One hour," Spetrovich nodded with a defeated sigh.

Nunez dropped into a renewed fit of laughter.

"I'll call your insurer immediately," Harlot replied, bothered by the accountant's drunken reaction.

"Thank you," I smiled.

I grabbed a black t-shirt and put it on as Nunez continued to laugh.

"What's so goddamned funny?!" Ronns irritably barked.

A bit red-faced, the money launderer was having trouble breathing. We had to wait for him to regain his composure. During that time, I put on a gray pair of street sneakers and laced them up.

"Cly?" Nunez finally managed to ask. "Could you save me for last?"

I could tell that Ronns and Spetrovich didn't understand his question—but Harlot did. Her eyes thoughtfully narrowed in my direction as I simply stood there and listened.

"Mr. Cly, or whatever the fuck his real name is, clearly has a history," Nunez insisted as he pointed a left index finger at me. "I'm thinking we've forced him back into his old lifestyle."

"Don't tell me you're scared of this fat piece of shit!" Spetrovich snorted.

Nunez's smile died as he looked over at the Russian.

"Someone's gonna piss him off," he warned them. "When that day comes, Cly's gonna be his old, lethal self again."

I kept my face blank, quietly hoping that it wouldn't get that far. Fortunately, the other crooks regarded Nunez skeptically—even Harlot.

"Perhaps you've had a bit too much to drink, Mr. Nunez?" Harlot suggested.

"Maybe I have," the accountant acknowledged. "But I was sober enough to watch this guy make a half-billion dollars in his *fucking underwear*!"

The guy had a point. Nunez looked over at Ronns.

"Someday, for some reason, Cly's gonna make us all dead. I wanna see how that happens, which I can't do if Cly kills me first."

"Cly's not stupid enough to try us," Ronns quietly argued, annoyed by Nunez's argument. "Besides, he's no threat to us."

"True," I admitted as I slowly—carefully—drew both Glocks from their rear holsters.

By the time my guns came out, Ronns' SIG was already drawn and aimed at my head. Spetrovich had jumped out of his chair and tapped his gadget belt. We all looked his way as a transparent force shield flared on. Unafraid, Nunez gave them an "I-told-you-so" smile. Harlot's serving wench was locked into a fighting stance, with a cybergun muzzle now visible under each palm.

Harlot merely sat there with a kill order at the tip of her tongue.

I took a deep breath and shook my head at all this drama.

"People, if I was this mythical badass, I would've killed Seamus myself," I glanced at Ronns as I simultaneously ejected the Glocks' mags. "Instead I'm here, begging for mercy. Technically, I got it: a second chance."

I shrugged as I set the guns on the table and stepped back one pace.

"You know what, folks? I'm not gonna fuck it up."

As I reached down and unbuckled my gun belt, I noticed that Ronns still hadn't lowered his pistol. Spetrovich sat down with a smirk (even though his force shield was still up). The serving gal/cyborg kept her weapons trained on me.

I turned to Nunez with a slow, determined smile.

"No Carlos, I plan to do what no one's ever done in this city before."

"And what's that?" Harlot asked, her poker face on maximum.

I dropped my gun belt on the table with a thoughtful sigh.

"I'm gonna own the crime fighting game in this town."

CHAPTER SEVEN

Word traveled fast on this boat.

By the time I reached *The Depravity's* one and only dance spot (*The Whoremonger's Club*), folks were cheering me on. Some were happy about Seamus' death. Others were amazed I had walked out of that room with a pulse and a sizeable fortune.

Then there were the leeches.

Guys offered me free drinks and an array of investment ideas. Women propositioned me under the techno-howl of whatever shitty remix the DJ was playing in the background. I politely told them all to fuck off. Then I snagged myself a bottled water and found a corner table.

Popularity wasn't a problem for me when I was a fixer. Everyone knew who I was but steered clear until they needed something. Since I didn't flaunt my wealth or abilities, I was underestimated by most—which might've saved my life tonight. As far as the mob bosses knew, I wasn't a threat and should be dead in a matter of days. Once they figured out I won't die so easily, they might take turns trying to kill me . . .

In which case, I will save Nunez for last.

My enemies—old and new—would be an issue. Now that the dust was settling, they'd see me as vulnerable. I needed gear, weapons, and a bunch of safe houses. With the price tag on my head, finding reliable allies would be tricky business. The most important thing was to reacquire power—and fast. Without some sort of influence, leverage, and/or status, I was a dead man walking.

The acquisition of power was why I got into the game in the first place. True power wasn't about being the biggest or the strongest. It was based on a combination of need and fear. As a fixer, my clientele needed discreet, reliable solutions to their varied problems. Being useful to them gave me power.

Also, I didn't have to be inherently dangerous to be feared. I simply paid other people to be dangerous in my name, which earned me the respect and fear any fixer would want. Had I been more of a "people" person, I could've started my own mob. Still, I found this bizarre turn of events to be a bit . . . liberating.

Yes, my empire was ash but I also didn't have to maintain it anymore. Doing so required eighteen-hour days with far too many obligations. I could leave my clients and contractors to either wither or prosper on their own. There weren't any bills to pay or jobs to manage. To stay alive, I had to forge an honest life with a different brand of power to it.

In a town this corrupt, that could be a violent kind of fun.

There I sat, alone with my thoughts when some guy limped through the crowd and headed toward me. In his late 30's, he easily stood out from the stylish revelers. He had a large build—maybe 6'4"—with more muscle than gut. A sloppy mane of blonde hair partially-obscured his scarred, bearded face. There was a silver wedding band squeezing the ring finger of his big left hand. His black clothing and matching woolen coat were loose enough to hide a gun or three.

I couldn't place the name but I remembered that face. An aging ex-con? A local cop, perhaps? I gazed him and confirmed that he was human. If he was street muscle, his luck must've gone south. Any enforcer with means would've had a healer fix his face (or at least that gimp in his left leg). Most guys his age would've either earned their way into a better-paying line of crime or given it up altogether. This guy looked low-rent.

What was his name?

As he came closer, I suddenly realized that I was kind of helpless. No armor. No guns. No contractors. Yeah, I could metalform but I didn't want to tip my hand—not yet. Besides, I shouldn't have to worry. The promise of merciless death ought to deter anyone from killing me on Triad turf. But everyone wasn't sane enough to play by those rules.

I kicked on Harlot's power, ready to "logic" him to death if I had to.

He stopped within easy striking distance.

"You're late," he said over the music.

"Excuse me?" I asked.

"I was babysitting your one o'clock," he explained with clear irritation. "She got tired of waiting and sent me to find you."

Ah yes. Grace.

I looked down at my new watch (a cheap timepiece provided after my Rolex was confiscated). Anyway, it was 2:08 a.m.

"She's not my problem anymore."

"Go to where you first met her. Do it now."

"I'm out of the game," I insisted with a friendly smile, ready to kill him if I had to.

"She knows about your current situation . . . and doesn't care."

It wasn't threatening. His tone was urgent, compelling, and scared. He sought me out because Grace needed more help than he could give her. Well tough shit. I wasn't a fixer anymore.

"If it's illegal, I can't touch it," I shrugged, pleased with the logic of the excuse.

The enforcer nervously looked around for a moment.

"She said you'd punk out," he frowned as his hard brown eyes roved the room. "That's why she also said that if you didn't meet her within the next hour, she'll be too dead to save the city."

I sized up his body language as I sipped my water. He wasn't lying. Not even a little.

"The threat's real, Mr. Cly," he said. "So you're coming with me. Right now. I've got too many family and friends here to –"

The gimp was interrupted as a flurry of gunshots exited through his chest. I had already thrown myself out of my chair while my table was chewed up by incoming pistol fire. As bullets punched through him, the dying bastard half-drew a snub-nosed .44 revolver. Instead of trying to fire back, he weakly tossed it my way. I caught it as he hit the floor.

I scrambled behind a lacquered column, which barely provided enough cover. Then I looked over at Grace's friend. He stared at me, silently pleading as he breathed his last . . .

Not bad, whoever you were.

There was a pause in the shooting. I rose to a single-kneed crouch and cocked the hammer. Being a "crime fighter," I didn't have to play harmless anymore. Besides, I needed to see if I still had my killer's touch. I aimed left at a small-breasted white woman with a short caramel dress and a 9-mil Beretta that she was busy reloading. I put a round between those small tits, watched her fall, and then searched for the other shooter(s).

My eyes zeroed in on her partner, who was tossing away his empty pistol with an angry snarl. His mustached lips cursed me as he went for another gun. The huge, chocolate-skinned hitman was dressed like a color-coated disco refugee—complete with a huge 'fro. Still, I couldn't laugh at the P-90 submachine gun he pulled out from under his red leather jacket. I could've let him raise his gun before I shot him but that would've been fair. And we don't fight fair in this town.

The .44 barked twice.

He fell backwards with a bullet in his stomach. His screams were drowned out by those of the terrified partygoers in the background. I stayed put and counted to ten, just in case there were any other shooters. At nine, a bunch of Triad guys charged in—all human. Dressed in black suits and matching shirts, they brandished assorted firearms and an eagerness to inflict violence.

I stood up and headed for the wounded shooter.

Along the way, I ignored the Triad boys and stepped over a screaming blonde (with a thigh wound). The Wung guys spotted me and rushed over. By then, I had reached the second shooter who helplessly glared up at me. I kicked his weapon away. The music was abruptly—and mercifully—cut. People were running for the doors or huddled in the background, too scared to run away.

"On the ground!" One of Harlot's men yelled with a thick Chinese accent.

I didn't move.

He jammed the barrel of his shotgun against my lower spine. My right hand reversed the grip on the .44. Then I spun around his line of fire and pistol-whipped him across the jaw. The move was so fast and brutal that the Triad shooter dropped without pulling the trigger. I lowered the gun as his pals aimed for my vital organs.

They knew who I was but just didn't care. Technically, they could reason, I had violated my Community Service by knocking their guy out. Triggers were caressed by the fingers of calloused killers. I tapped into Harlot's stolen power.

"I thought you were supposed to protect your paying customers!" I angrily shouted. "I've just been attacked by two assassins. Me! A paying guest!"

I glared down at the unconscious Triad goon on the floor.

"Then this asshole sticks a shotgun in my back?!" I yelled. "Damn right I knocked him out!"

Eyes thoughtfully narrowed as Harlot's power rushed over them. I tossed the .44 to the floor and spread my arms out wide.

"Go ahead," I dared them. "Shoot me! If you're lucky, Harlot won't kill your kids. She'll just feed you to Kristos!"

Guns quickly lowered. One of the pricks pulled out a radio and called for a healer. Satisfied, I turned around and stomped on the black hitman's balls. He groaned under the extra pain. I looked him over again. Like his dead partner, the guy was human.

If this schmuck was a freelancer, he probably didn't even know who hired him. Still, it would be dumb of me not to ask . . . especially when I could be so "logical" and all.

"Give me a name and I'll cut you loose," I lied.

"Fuck you!" The triggerman yelled with a noticeably French accent.

"If you don't, my Asian friends will hurt you worse than I have," I warned him. "Now talk to me and save your life."

Through his pain, the hitman glared up at me for several seconds. His mouth twitched as he fought Harlot's power. Then he looked over at his dead partner. Something in his expression changed when he looked back at me. Tears of sorrow crept out of his hate-filled eyes. Damn! They were lovers. His grief was so powerful that it would temporarily shield his mind from her influence.

"You won't break me!" He defiantly laughed. "And your one o'clock's gonna die alone!"

As he kept laughing, the fucker showed off his big pearly-whites. I noticed a gold tooth on the lower-left side of his jaw line. Only, it wasn't gleaming in the overhead lighting. It was flashing a gold-hued pulse –

"Bomb!" I yelled.

The nearest cover was one of the club's three bars. I really needed to go metalform. Instead, I ran. With the bar some twenty feet away, I knew I wouldn't make it. I got halfway there when the asshole's bomb tooth exploded. The blast lifted me off my feet and into the customer side of the bar. Ribs snapped on my right side. I dropped to the floor amidst new screams of fear and pain. While not as bad as a bomb vest, the exploding tooth did its job.

Through my own pain and ringing ears, I rolled onto my good side and took it all in. Four Triad boys were ripped apart and clearly dead. Three more were fucked up and writhing on the floor. The other six had gotten clear and were setting up a perimeter around the suicide bomber's smoldering remains. From the waist-down, he was charred. From the waist-up, he was . . . gooey.

The violence took me back to the 90's. Back then, I was in Desert Storm up to my neck in Iraqi cyber soldiers and WMDs.

Fun times.

I blacked out with a smile –

Then I woke up screaming.

A skinny, old healer-bitch grinned down at me with yellowed teeth. Dressed in blue medical scrubs, her wizened hands were *inside* my bare chest. Healers!

Some touched you and your body regenerated, usually in a matter of minutes. Others put their hands through your skin, much like it was water. While the latter version healed you within seconds, the process hurt like hell.

"You are whole," she replied in broken English.

I frowned at my t-shirt, which had been cut open while I was down. I felt better the instant she pulled her hands out of me. I sat up and got rid of the ruined t-shirt. A surly Triad grunt tossed me a gray replacement. Before I put it on, I glanced at my watch. Only five minutes had passed since I got laid out, which meant that Harlot's crew members were a scary brand of efficient. I stood up and gave the short old healer a grateful peck on the forehead.

Then I looked around.

Debris and bodies were hastily being cleared away by thirty guys who looked exactly alike. Probably a duplicator: a sub-class super capable of making dozens of copies of himself. Short and lean, he/they looked to be Chinese, wore the same dark green coveralls, and wielded assorted tools. I had the nagging suspicion that *The Whoremonger's Club* would be as good as new within the next twelve hours or so.

Harlot stormed into the room and headed my way. She looked pissed enough for both of us and probably needed someone to shout at. I sighed as the healer bowed toward Harlot and headed for the nearest door.

"Get off my ship!" Harlot seethed.

I had to admit her anger was something of a turn-on right now.

"I'm fine, Harlot. Thanks for asking," I replied with a fake smile.

She wasn't amused.

"All types of mayhem are about to descend upon you. You will not be on *The Depravity* when that happens!"

That sounded ominous.

"What do you mean?"

She grabbed my left arm and started to briskly walk me toward the nearest corridor. A pair of Triad goons followed us.

"As word about your new 'status' continues to spread, we've received word that multiple bounties have been placed on your head."

"Value?" I frowned.

"The largest one was $50 million—for your head in a bag. We expect that figure to rise."

I softly whistled.

"You don't have contractors to defend you anymore, Mr. Cly," Harlot flatly stated. "In fact, I'd wager that you'll be dead by Monday."

I didn't have a good answer for that so I kept silent. We stepped through a door, down a bunch of corridors, and enjoyed a brief elevator ride. Everyone we passed gave us a wide, nervous berth. Maybe it was because of Harlot's mood. Or perhaps, they didn't want to be in the line of fire when someone else tried to kill me.

We made a few more turns and then came upon another pair of black-suited goons standing guard at a closed hatchway door. My suitcase was waiting nearby. Just beyond the door was the faint smell of seawater. As we approached, the door self-opened inward.

"Your account's been arranged," Harlot stiffly stated. "You'll find a detailed file of your finances in the suitcase. Once you're ashore, you'll find a cab waiting for you with the fare already paid."

"I apologize for the disorder I have caused," I replied with a low, formal bow. "I'm in your debt."

The veteran crook paused, her anger somewhat muted by my show of respect. Then she reluctantly returned the gesture.

"So who were the shooters?"

"Freelancers, most likely," Harlot replied. "I suspect that they were out to collect your head before anyone else could."

Nah. Freelancers would know better than to try a hit on Triad turf—even out-of-towners. They'd wait for me to leave the ship and then kill me. Instead, these two threw their lives away on a public hit, which made no sense. Even if they did manage to kill me, they never would've made it off *The Depravity.*

Also, freelancers don't commonly invest in suicide implants. My guess was that the female shooter had one too. Then there was the part where the hitman indirectly mentioned Grace, which would only make sense if they had her under surveillance.

No. These two were loyal to someone or some group.

"What about the guy they killed?"

"According to his ID, his name was Peter Ratiapp. Did you know him?"

I shook my head.

"Did he have family?"

"Yes," Harlot replied.

"Give him a decent burial and send me the bill," I sighed. "He saved my life."

"Consider it done," Harlot replied. "Good luck, Mr. Cly."

I gave her a grateful nod, picked up my suitcase, and headed for the exit. Below was a short floating stairwell, which led to a dark-blue cigarette boat. A burly Latino was at the wheel. Dressed in gray fatigue pants and a white wife-beater, he had look of "smuggler" about him. Three of Harlot's goons waited near the aft section of the vessel, where its four side-by-side engines purred in the water.

"One more thing, Mr. Cly," Harlot shouted over the engines.

I stopped and faced her. Her demeanor had turned pure Dragon Lady.

"You will be watched," she promised me. "Stray from the terms of your Community Service and you'll end up far worse than the late Vincent Mockre."

CHAPTER EIGHT

"You don't have contractors to defend you anymore, Mr. Cly," Harlot's words echoed in my seething mind. *"In fact, I'd wager that you'll be dead by Monday."*

Harlot had just tried to fucking kill me . . . again!

I replayed the words in my head a few more times before I was certain. As the cigarette boat raced toward Pillar City, I glared back at *The Depravity*. The clever bitch wanted me to believe—truly believe—that I didn't have a chance in hell of surviving the weekend. Backed by her power, those two little sentences would've tainted my every decision.

Maybe I'd make a string of stupid mistakes and prove her right. Or perhaps, I'd feel an overwhelming sense of despair and put a bullet in my head. Either way, I would've had a tag on my toe by Tuesday morning. Of course, I couldn't prove any of this—but that's the elegance of Harlot's power.

I flipped open my suitcase and inventoried my wares. The clothes were still there. A white banking folder was added, as promised. I borrowed a flashlight from one of my Triad escorts. Skimming through the documents, my current account balance was $215,670,412.37. After the EDR's 10% fee, the number should've been an even $216 mil. Then I noticed the invoice for repairs to *The Whoremonger's Club*.

Ah. That.

Also in the folder was a wad of c-notes, wrapped in rubber bands. I quickly unwrapped it and counted out two grand. I folded it up and stuck it in my front left pocket. The folder contained a red-and-black debit card for a bank in Hong Kong. I slid it into my wallet. Then I memorized the relevant details of my EDR account before pitching my banking documents into the water.

After pocketing the wallet, I looked for anything else of interest. Clothes, underwear, and toiletries made up the rest of my luggage.

Now that I had money, I needed high-end gear and weaponry—both of which would be harder to find. Not only did I have to acquire them legally, I had to find someone crazy enough to sell them to me (and risk dying in the crossfire). Then there was the matter of replacement armor. I needed something comparable to my old suit (or better). Samir could come through on everything I needed—assuming I could track him down in time. The elusive armorer rarely stayed in the same place for very long.

The hardest part would be to arrange my "re-introduction" into the mean streets of Pillar City. Past victims of Community Service doomed themselves by hiding out by day and fighting crime at night. That wouldn't work in Downtown, where your rep made (or killed) you. If I didn't control my "crime fighting brand" my enemies would do it for me.

The boat dropped me off at a vacant concrete dock. One of the Triad goons tossed me a burner phone and told me to expect a call within two days. That followed. I was supposed to sign away my assets and they needed a way to reach me. Missing my tricked-out Smartphone, I slipped its cheap replacement into my right pocket as the boat left the dock.

Beyond it was an empty asphalt parking lot with a waiting yellow cab and no nearby cover. As I watched the cigarette boat race off into the night, I resisted the urge to look for snipers. Then I picked up the suitcase and calmly headed for the cab, which slowly rolled toward me.

The driver was a tired old black guy who reeked of cigarettes. Short and wrinkled, he dressed shabbily and looked so very typical. It was a damned-convincing disguise. My gaze allowed me to see that he was really an augmented faceshifter with some beastshifter abilities. With those powers, I wouldn't be a cabbie.

I'd be a killer.

I couldn't recall any local hitters with those two abilities. Yesterday, I might've even tried to hire him. With those powers, my would-be killer could look like anyone, any animal, or a bit of both.

I once knew a shifter who worked her way through college doing water shows as a "mermaid" at *SeaWorld*. Half-beastial shapeshifting's a tricky thing though. It required a lot more concentration than just beastshifting or faceshifting alone. Still, this fucker could sprout claws and tear me to shreds—if I let him.

"Want me to put that in the trunk for you, sir?"

"Please," I replied with a smile.

"Right away, sir," the fucker nodded as he pressed the trunk release.

The real cabbie's corpse was probably folded in there with a bullet in his head. I waited for the shifter to pull a gun on me. Instead, he left the keys in the ignition, opened the driver's side door, and got out. That was surprising. All he really had to do was shoot me through the door (I would've). I guess he was a more hands-on type of guy.

I stepped up to hand over the suitcase with my left hand.

"Careful," I grinned, "it's a bit heavy."

"I'll manage," he smiled back.

As he took the suitcase by its handle, my left hand brushed against his right. I kept a straight face as I snagged his powers. The shifter immediately began to revert to his true form as he turned around and headed toward the trunk. Now he was a white guy, with shoulder-length black hair and a muscular build. The killer felt his clothes get tighter as he grew back to his true height, which was around 6'1".

I pretended to look shocked.

"What the hell?!" I convincingly yelped.

Confused, he dropped the suitcase and spun around. The shifter's real face was uglier than mine with a fat nose and some missing teeth. His left eye was blue and his right one was green. He noticed his pale hands, glared up at me –

– and got front-kicked in the balls.

"Nice try!" I yelled as he staggered away.

Clearly, I hadn't kicked him hard enough. Annoyed that he wasn't on the ground, I rushed him. Yeah, I could've ended this fight in under three seconds and in a hundred different ways. Instead, I slammed him into the cab. When he still didn't drop, I followed up with a punch to the balls. Half-dazed, the shifter slid sideways, against the driver's side door, then dropped to his face.

"That's what happens when you buy cheap augments!" I taunted as I kicked him in ribs a bunch of times.

Then I knelt and rolled him over.

"Who sent you?!" I yelled.

The stubborn killer growled as he tried to wrestle me down. I drove both of my thumbs into his eyes, which made him let me go. Then I shot up to my feet and stomped on his face a few times. What a waste! I could've used Harlot's power to fucking recruit the guy (or at least get some answers out of him). But with Harlot's people watching me, I had to play the fucking role of "incompetent ex-fixer."

Besides, this guy was semi-pro, at best.

Breathing hard, I wiped some sweat off my brow. Blinded and bruised, the shifter coughed up blood. He knew what was coming next. I think he was about to try and beg. That's when I stomped on his exposed windpipe. Then I stomped on his sternum because that's what an amateur might do.

My smoker's lungs weren't up for the exertion and forced me into a bout of coughing. I pulled out my pack of Marlboros and tossed them into the cab. While I still had the moves, my stamina and striking power were downright pathetic. That would have to change.

All-in-all, I think my performance was adequate. Anyone watching would figure that I wasn't a real threat. I'd appear to be too rattled to make the shifter tell me who sent him (Harlot). Hopefully, my invisible audience also believed that his power had collapsed. The thing about augments (cheap or not) was that they could always fail when used too often. Having lived with the specter of augmentation failure myself, I could relate.

Bothered by this second attempt on my life, I pulled out the burner phone. I pulled up the phone's number and committed it to memory. Then I tossed the phone onto the shifter's corpse. I patted down the shifter and found nothing but a pack of Newport 100's. Out of curiosity, I decided to check the cab's open trunk. I peered inside . . . and was glad that Anywhere wasn't with me. This definitely would've made him puke.

The inside of the trunk was lined with clear, bloodstained plastic. The real cabbie was laid out in wide-eyed death. He only wore black dress socks and a soiled pair of white briefs. His throat was clawed open and his stomach had been chewed out within the last few hours.

Better him than me.

There was a black garbage bag next to the corpse. Inside it, I found a slutty pink dress, black purse, and a pair of black high heels, all clean and smelling of cheap perfume. The shifter's purse was empty: a mere prop and nothing else. The twisted fucker (in the guise of a fine-assed woman) must've seduced the cabbie. The dirty old man couldn't turn down free pussy and obliged "her," only to end up a Happy Meal.

Finding the cabbie's clothes at the bottom of the trash bag, I emptied his pockets to find a cell phone, wallet, and almost eighty bucks in small bills. I replaced his wallet's contents with my own and then put it in my back pocket. I also kept his watch and phone. I slammed the trunk shut, turned around, and walked away.

As I briskly left the murder scene, I expected to get attacked from any direction. My eyes drifted from one building to another. Mostly small warehouses and machine shops, everything around here looked to be closed for the night. After three blocks, I pulled out of the cell phone and dialed the number for the burner phone Harlot's guy had given me. I wasn't the least bit surprised to hear a violent explosion three blocks away.

Cute, Harlot. Very cute.

CHAPTER NINE

I needed to get to Grace—fast. I just hoped she hadn't gotten herself killed by now.

After hiking eight blocks, I lucked out and flagged down another cab. This time the driver was a plump old lady who looked human and barely gave me a second glance. I told her to head for Downtown's red light district. She grunted and headed for Underpass 4. The six-lane, spiral highway was one of four, each linking Uptown to Downtown. Even this late at night, traffic was buzzing.

Twenty minutes later, the cabbie dropped me off next to *The Slutty Minx Motel's* giant, 60's-era neon sign. The gaudy thing was shaped like a blue-and-pink pastel bow tie on two white rusting support beams. Underneath the larger sign was a smaller VACANCY sign that flashed in red neon. I paid and exited the cab, feeling like Bambi during deer season.

As the cab rolled off, I kicked on the metalform and faceshifting powers in unison. The bizarre shift was holding—for now. Although I looked like my flesh-and-blood self, I was really solid titanium. Better still, I was tough enough to get run over by a bus and strong enough to flip it over.

I looked up at the two-story, U-shaped motel that had about one hundred rooms. The parking lot was packed, which didn't surprise me. *The Slutty Minx* was a popular hangout for sexual deviants, druggies, and adulterers. It was the type of place where you needed to wear gloves before washing your hands and the roaches spoke three languages. The allure was two-fold: you could pay in cash and everyone minded their own business.

All in all, it was an adequate meeting spot.

Grace and I first met here in '02, a few months before her coma. An old college pal of hers (Anita something) came to Uptown on business and disappeared. The police had no leads because her abductors routinely paid them not to find any. Grace knew that Anita would end up dead—or worse—without some back-end help.

When she grudgingly came to me, I didn't mind asking around . . . but not for free. Unfortunately, Grace was an honest cop with modest means. We settled on a price for my services, in the form of a "big, painful favor" some day. Grace grudgingly agreed.

I made some calls and tracked down Anita within a few hours. Her abductors were human traffickers from Jersey with an efficient little export operation. They snatched American gals, doped them up, and then shipped them overseas. Grace's friend (and nine other abductees) were about to get flown off to Kuwait.

Luckily, the traffickers weren't mob-affiliated and realized that I'd make a bad enemy. A few more phone calls, some wrangling, and *voila*! The missing Anita what's-her-name was returned that same day. Yeah, the poor dear was a sobbing, strung-out mess but she wasn't too far-gone to save. Grace asked about the other victims. I told her that I didn't bother with them as the deal was only for Anita. Mission accomplished. Roll credits.

My lack of concern for the other victims disgusted Grace's moral sensibilities. What really bothered her was that she couldn't save the others or bring the traffickers to justice. Had she managed to get a warrant and raid the place, Grace knew her superiors would've tipped off the traffickers. Even if (by some miracle) they were to get busted, the D.A.'s office would "lose" the case—for a fee. In a town this dirty, Grace had to settle on saving her friend.

I had forgotten about that "big, painful favor" that she owed me. Maybe I'd –

"You're late," Grace said from behind me.

I turned around and sized her up. The years had been kind. At forty-five, the psi-hacker still looked a bit south of forty and stood a few inches taller than me. Though she wasn't a cop anymore, Grace stuck with her old work attire.

She sported a navy-blue pantsuit, light-green blouse, fingerless black leather gloves, and stylish steel-toed dress boots with the low heels. Her brown hair was tied up in a frizzy ponytail that only had a few strands of gray to hint at her real age. Her attractive, makeup-free face looked extra stressed tonight.

As usual, Grace kept five guns on her person. Two Glock 9s were parallel-holstered against her shapely hips. Two more were in a double chest holster rig, keeping her decent rack company. The fifth gun—an Uzi—was gripped in her right hand. She held the barrel mere inches from my nose. I raised my hands in a mock gesture of surrender.

"Sorry," I shrugged. "I had to kill a few people."

"I heard," Grace grimly replied.

Her guilty, hazel eyes roved across my torso.

"What?" I lowered my arms.

Grace tapped my chest with the Uzi's barrel.

"The Wung's healer slipped a tracker bomb in your chest when she was patching you up on *The Depravity*."

That remark left me speechless for a moment.

"You disarmed it, right?"

"Yeah. Right after you beat that shapeshifter to death," Grace replied. "If his augment hadn't given out, he would have had you for dessert."

"Yeah," I replied with fake modesty. "Lucky me."

So, the psi-hacker had been keeping tabs on me. That meant she cracked *The Depravity's* firewalls and tapped directly into their cameras—something my best people knew they couldn't do.

"So, the Wungs hired him to kill me?"

Grace shook her head.

"The shifter's last five hits were all paid for by the O'Flernans," she explained. "He was wrapping up a job in a Queens when he received a text from Ronns, offering eight million reasons to kill you."

I wasn't surprised in the least.

"But the Wungs still want me dead," I insisted.

"True," Grace nodded. "And they weren't in much of a hurry. All they had to do was trigger that bomb in your chest and you'd have been chunks. Then there was the cell phone bomb, which I jammed until you dialed up the number."

She had a point. I guess Harlot wanted to give Ronns' guy the first crack at me. When he failed, her people tried to blow me up—twice. The Wungs and the O'Flernans had just risen to the top of my shit list. When this was over, I'd have to have a little fun at their expense.

"Thanks."

"You're welcome," Grace replied. "Just remember that the bomb's lodged against your sternum. One good hit might set it off."

"Guess I'll need more surgery," I mused aloud.

Then I frowned.

"This bomb in my chest," I said as I tapped my sternum. "It was recording everything I said and did too?"

"No. But you've got plenty of tiny cameras sewn into your clothing, belt, and shoes."

"So I'm like a Christmas tree? Only, instead of lights, I have cameras?"

"Something like that," Grace replied. "I've deactivated those."

"Thanks."

She nodded with a sad, guilty sigh.

"What?" I asked.

"I saw Pete die through those cameras," she said. "He was married . . . third kid on the way. I almost had to pry him from his daughter's arms yesterday."

I could've advised Grace to leave her conscience at home but she wouldn't listen. Such was the curse of being a good person.

Well, time for haggling.

"Okay, what's this about?" I asked. "Ratiapp mentioned something about a threat?"

"We'll talk inside," Grace insisted.

Grace led. I followed.

We reached a flight of concrete stairs and began our ascent. As I stepped onto the second floor, I felt like we were being watched. Judging from the way Grace occasionally glanced at the parking lot below, she did too.

"How many people know you're in town?"

"Too many," she replied.

We stopped in front of Room #204. She pulled a key from her back pocket and unlocked the door.

"What the hell?!" Grace groaned with frustrated annoyance as she stepped into the room and looked around.

"What?" I frowned as I closed the door behind me.

Everything looked normal enough. The seedy motel room had a queen-sized bed with a white comforter. The brown carpet had seen more than its fair share of cigarette burns and unidentifiable stains. The white walls and ceiling could use a fresh coat of paint. There was a fairly new flat screen TV mounted on a small dresser in one corner of the room. On the opposite side was a round wooden table with two wooden chairs.

The only things out of place were the six large duffel bags next to the nightstand. On one of the bags was a folded-up piece of paper with Grace's name on it. She walked over and picked it up. The more she read, the darker her expression became.

"Something wrong?"

"They left town!" Grace shook her head with disgust as she crumpled the note and slid it into her pocket. "Mitch and Seth. They . . . they promised to help me out."

I locked and chained the door. Grace sat at the foot of the bed and fought back tears as she looked over at the bags.

"Okay, Grace," I began, "why am I here?"

Grace looked up at me with clear reluctance.

"I need your help."

"What are you into?" I asked.

"That's not your concern," Grace stiffly replied as she stood up and gave the room's tiny bathroom a quick once-over. Then she tossed the Uzi on the bed, reached into her jacket, and pulled out a small digital recorder.

"I'm here about D'Angelo Gratte. He runs one of your shell companies."

I didn't bother to ask the psi-hacker how she knew about *Lairs 'R Us*. Nor was I in the mood to lie about it. Under different circumstances, I'd actually brag. My little shell company catered to the remodeling needs of wealthy geeks. Just last week, Gratte did a job for some chucklehead who wanted to make his basement to look like the bridge of the *U.S.S. Enterprise* (the J.J. Abrams version). Gratte's group traveled the globe and was well-known in the sci-fi community. Their legit jobs actually netted me a decent profit.

But it was the illegal stuff that brought in the big cash.

Unofficially, Gratte's team built lairs (each suited to a client's individual needs). They've built nuke bunkers, safe houses, genetics labs, and even full-sized HQ's. If the money was real, no job was too big for *Lairs R' Us*. They weren't picky about their clientele either. They'd done work for numerous terror cells, intelligence agencies, super villains, and even the occasional super hero.

D'Angelo Gratte was the figurehead. Our business ties were a well-kept secret because some of his clients didn't like me very much. If the wrong people knew that he worked for me, things could get bloody in a hurry. I discreetly covered his expenses—always in cash. If I wanted any of his properties for my firm's use, I'd simply pose as a customer.

As I thought on this, I realized that I had a new problem. In less than 24 hours, Nunez would use my accounting files to back trace the names of every shell company I owned. If Spetrovich really managed to steal the *Lairs R. Us* expense files, I was a dead man. The four mobs would shit lead when they realized that I knew the specs on over half the lairs in town—most of which belonged to them.

Grace hit the recorder's PLAY button.

"Benjamin Cly," my voice answered.

"We hit the mother lode, boss!" Gratte's voice triumphantly yelled over the background noise of breaching tools. His Burroughs accent was unmistakable.

I gave Grace a true "fuck-you" glare. She was tapping my encrypted calls and didn't seem to care if I knew. Yesterday, I would've killed her. Today, I couldn't do much more than have a hissy fit. Tomorrow, however . . .

"Pray tell," my voice urged.

"Someone's already built a lair down here!" Gratte continued.

"How do you know?"

"We were digging out the swimming pool when we found a bona fide escape tunnel!"

"Whose lair is it?" I asked.

"No idea," Gratte giggled with the ecstasy of a seasoned looter. "Once we cut our way in through the tunnel we're gonna find out!"

"Anti-intrusion measures?"

"None yet," Gratte replied. "But we'll have this sorted out by morning."

"Do nothing. Touch nothing," I ordered.

"Aw c'mon, Cly!" Gratte whined. "This ain't the first lair I've ever found, y'know!"

"Sorry, Gratte," I sighed. "But there's no rush, right? Let's be careful on this one."

"Yeah-yeah."

"Secure the site. No one goes in without my approval."

Gratte muttered something in Italian.

"Understood," he replied before hanging up.

Grace hit the STOP button.

"That's why you're here, Grace?" I asked with pure sarcasm. "You need a lair? Something with a fireplace and a solarium, perhaps?"

The psi-hacker put the recorder away.

"I need the address. That's all," Grace said with an urgent—no, desperate—look in her eye. The same look Ratiapp had before he died.

Had Gratte kept his address files on a computer, the bitch would've hacked them up and tried to sneak in there by now. But Gratte logged everything on paper, which could be quickly burned if necessary. Cutouts did the real estate transactions so that folks like Grace couldn't easily track down our acquisitions.

I paused to consider her request.

The lair rested under a three-story brick house in Uptown (1339 Highswick Drive). Set in the middle of an old-money neighborhood full of big houses, this one boasted four bedrooms and two bathrooms. It looked innocent enough to be turned into a prime piece of criminal real estate. A few weeks back, Gratte spotted it in the classifieds and got my go-ahead to buy it.

That was Wednesday.

If Gratte was right about a lair, it probably belonged to a hero. Most criminals who lived in Pillar City had mob ties and lived out in the open. The few local "super villains" (lunatics in costumes, really) commuted from New York or Jersey. Only a hero would feel the need for a secret hideout.

The house's previous owner was listed as a Vivian Hallett, a corporate consultant who mysteriously disappeared over a year ago. Hallett's brother had her declared dead and put the home on the market about a month back. The fucker was broke, divorced, and paying child support on two kids. Gratte took the place for a steal.

With the Mockre case coming to a close, I was about to unleash my researchers and figure out who the hell Hallett really was. There were still a lot of heroes running around back then. She could've been one of them. Depending on the condition of the facility, I might've kept it or sold the lair and its contents. Whatever was there might've ended up on the black market or kept for use in the field.

Things had changed.

I needed that lair like oxygen right now. There was no fucking way I'd hand that place—and its toys—over to Grace.

"I'm surprised you didn't track down Gratte."

"I tried," Grace frowned. "He and his entire team disappeared."

That was a problem.

"When?"

"Sometime yesterday," she shrugged.

"Any leads?"

"Just you."

Maybe they were working a last-minute job. Or someone had gone after them. If Gratte and his scavengers were killed, fine. If they were taken alive and tortured, I had problems. Gratte worked for me longer than any of my other contractors. He watched me build my firm from the ground-up and knew how it ticked. Community Service or not, I might have to kill him simply to protect my secrets.

"I'll take you there."

Grace scoffed at the idea.

"Is that a problem?" I asked with a nod toward the six bags. "Clearly, you planned on a four-person op. As far as I can see, you could use an extra set of hands."

"I've got a crisis situation and very little time left," she explained with waning patience. "The last thing I need is to look after a fixer with a death wish."

"Guess you didn't hear the latest word," I said as I folded my arms and smiled.

With a grin, I gave her a summary of tonight's brutal events, starting with the Irish wake. When I was done, Grace looked up at me with a mixture of awe and ridicule.

"So, do we have a deal?" I asked.

She stubbornly shook her head.

"Give me the address and we're done. I saved your life tonight –"

"You owe me," I cut in. "One for your college friend. And now this. If you're dead, I can't collect."

"I just saved you from being blown up—twice!" Grace countered.

Anyone else would've reactivated the bomb and threatened me. She just wasn't the type.

"Whatever," I sighed. "The point is that I'm not doing this for free."

Grace rolled her eyes.

"What do you want?"

Before I could reply, the sound of heavy footsteps approached from outside. Grace drew one of her Glocks and aimed for the door. Still in my aching, faceshifted metalform, I ignored the Uzi, figuring that my fists would do a lot more damage than mere bullets.

Seconds later, a huge bastard crashed through the door like it was a stiff curtain. His build was so massive that his shoulders brought the fucking door frame down. Bits of wall crumbled in his wake. It was almost intimidating.

Almost.

Before Grace could squeeze the trigger, I deftly stepped into her line of fire, while keeping my eyes on our unwanted guest.

"Cly, Are you crazy?!" she whispered. "He's a super!"

"No worries, Grace," I smiled and kicked on Harlot's power. "I got this."

CHAPTER TEN

I heard that costumes were making a comeback but this guy went way old school. The two-piece, red-and-black outfit was short-sleeved and clung to his broad 6'11" frame like a thin spandex hide. I guess he wanted to show off his muscles, which visibly bulged through the fabric. He was a bit south of 400 pounds with about zero-percent body fat.

I could smell his God-awful breath from across the room. Black boots ran up to his knees. His red belt had a scowling black skull for a buckle. Black gloves covered his enormous hands, which flexed their thick fingers with aggressive anticipation. With no weapons or gadgets to speak of, it was clear that this ape relied too much on his abilities—which I sized up with a glance.

I've killed better.

His costume didn't come with a mask, which was a shame because his face was uglier than mine. Bald-shaven head. Mean brown eyes. Yellowed teeth. The nose had a swollen, oft-broken look to it. His left ear was half-bitten away. Even though he was in his mid-30's, he was certainly an amateur.

I gave him a cold stare and waited for his move.

"Gimme the bitch," he growled with a deep, menacing voice.

Grace moved a few paces to my left, her Glock lowered and the hammer cocked.

"Try it," she threatened with a steely voice. "I'll just close my eyes and aim at your breath!"

The big guy merely smirked in reply but he missed her point. A bullet in the mouth just might kill him . . .

"Sorry chief," I cut in. "She's a bit grouchy tonight. For the record, who the hell are you?"

"SpineSnapper," he replied with a practiced sneer.

I blinked.

I tried to keep a straight face. Honestly.

Then I broke out laughing—the kind that takes a solid minute to control. The rude, tears-in-my-eyes kind. Couldn't help myself. I fell rump-first onto the edge of the bed. My concentration cracked so badly that I couldn't hold the metalform. If SpineSnapper had come at me then and there he'd have gotten me.

Instead, he actually looked like a hurt little child.

"I'm sorry!" I apologized, trying to breathe. "I shouldn't laugh! It's really rude –"

But then I broke into a renewed fit of laughter.

Grace, who was equally curious about what was so funny, shrugged at SpineSnapper. I regained my composure as the augment took an angry step my way, eager to kill me. I raised my hands in mock surrender. If he touched me, I'd tear his throat out with his own fucking power.

If he didn't, we'd talk . . . and then I'd kill him.

"Sorry," I managed to say. "I thought you knew that you were the fourth 'SpineSnapper' to hit the scene since 1981."

That stopped him in his tracks.

"What?!" he exclaimed as he reared back in Shatneresque shock.

"Didn't you check Wikipedia? Google?" I asked.

"No," he paused. "Why would I do that?"

I wiped the tears away, fought back more laughter, and then stood up.

"When you come up with a villain name, make sure it's unique," I advised.

"So, do I have to kill the other three SpineSnappers?"

"Nah," I shook my head. "The first one hung himself in the mid-80's. The second earned herself a ride to the gas chamber in the late 90's. I had the third one poisoned around 2002, which is why I know so much about the SpineSnapper legacy."

He clearly didn't want to switch names—even under the influence of Harlot's power. This SpineSnapper might've spent weeks (with a thick crayon) making up a list of "clever" villain nicknames—until he came up with that one.

"All supers?" SpineSnapper asked.

"Yep," I replied. "Which is the problem here. Now, if you want to keep the name, that's okay. But muscle alone won't get you respect on these streets. That, my friend, is a tricky thing."

"How do I do that?"

"Build your brand," I urged him. "If you started a major crime syndicate—that would be a game changer. So would picking up a scary power that has nothing to do with super strength. Imagine trying to fight a muscle guy with . . . a poisonous touch. Maybe a teleporter. Or one who could turn himself invisible? That's scary."

"But super strength is a cool power!" SpineSnapper objected.

"Yeah," I nodded. "But it's about as unique as a stick of gum."

That took the pride out of his sails as I folded my arms. Grace looked on, surprised that we weren't in a two-on-one fight to the death.

"About the most common powers are super strength, flight, and some kind of armored skin," I continued. "You have these powers, right?"

"Well," SpineSnapper dejectedly eyed the ceiling. "My skin's bulletproof. And I can bench 27.3 tons. But I can't fly. I'm saving up for that one."

"And that's the other thing."

"What?"

"Powers are like tits to me, y'know?" I argued gesturing outward with my hands. "I like 'em grand and I like 'em real."

SpineSnapper nodded with undersexed enthusiasm. Something told me that he had his sub-par genes altered (in part) to boost his odds at booty calls. Pity. He should've spent the money on a face replacement, breath spray, roofies, and a shiny new car. He might've gotten himself laid with change to spare.

"Don't get me wrong," I continued, "I've met me some damned-awesome augments in my day. But the natural-born ones are better because they've had their powers all their lives. They know 'em like they know their own faces. Get what I'm saying?"

The idiot frowned for a clueless eternity. Then he scowled down at me.

"Are you calling me a wannabe hood?!"

Absolutely, you dumb piece of . . .

"No!" I laughingly lied. "I'm just saying that, with your current powers, you've got an uphill climb to establish yourself as a legend in the crime game."

"Then I better start making my bones," SpineSnapper replied, back in full-asshole mode.

"You really don't want to –"

"Now get out of my way," he scowled. "Or I'll rip you in half!"

"Okay," I sighed.

SpineSnapper's face twisted with ugly confusion. He didn't expect me to give up so easily. Grace frowned and took a half-step back.

"What do you mean 'okay'?!" Grace hissed.

"I tried to talk some sense into him," I shook my head. "But if he wants to do this the hard way . . ."

The bruiser cracked his knuckles, generating an impressive sound.

"Why should I be afraid of a worthless little man like you?" SpineSnapper asked.

That insult stung a bit. Maybe it had something to do with the recent theft of my multi-billion-dollar empire. I forced out an angry sigh as I went for my wallet. SpineSnapper curiously frowned as I pulled out one of my business cards. I held it out in the palm of my right hand. The fucker hesitated for a moment.

"It's just a card," I said evenly.

SpineSnapper took the card. When his hand touched mine, I took away his strength and hardened skin. While he looked the same, the big man was only human now. Given time, all of that muscle would've faded away.

"Benjamin Cly & Associates—Crisis Management Services," SpineSnapper read aloud.

Then he winced.

"It says here that you're the owner/operator?"

He looked up from the card with saucer-wide eyes.

"Wait! You're *the* Benjamin Cly?! The fixer?"

"That's me."

Grace turned her head toward the nearest wall to hide her grin. SpineSnapper was terrified. Maybe he didn't want to become one of the untold thousands of people my organization's killed over the years. I simply looked up at him in menacing silence.

"Y-You got it wrong, Mr. Cly!" SpineSnapper pleaded, his voice no longer deep. He actually sounded a bit nerdy. "I want to work for you! That's why I got myself augmented."

I bit back a snicker.

"Come again?"

"My mom died and left me some insurance money," he said. "After taxes, it came to three hundred grand."

"I hope you buried her someplace nice," I reproachfully replied.

"Of course! She was my mom," SpineSnapper nodded, his hands searching for pockets to hide in. Too bad his costume didn't have any.

"Good. Continue."

"Well," he paused, "I wanted to be a super hero since I was a kid. But these days, that's just like suicide. So I figured I'd be a henchman –"

"You mean 'henchperson'," Grace corrected him.

I resisted the urge to tell her to shut the fuck up. This was my bluff and I didn't need her help with it.

"Oh! Sorry," SpineSnapper apologized to Grace. "*Henchperson*. So I bought some augments. Got a costume online and—"

"And now you're out to make a name for yourself, eh?" I asked, hoping that he'd get to the point before I died of hunger.

"Yeah," SpineSnapper nodded. "The bounty on your, uh, friend was going toward a down payment on a lair, a flight power package, and maybe some dental work."

"You don't say?" I asked, while giving Grace a quick glance. She went tense real fast. "And what's my 'friend' worth these days?"

"Ten million alive. Two million dead," SpineSnapper replied. "Everyone's looking for her, last I heard."

Someone wanted Grace and had deep enough pockets to make that happen. This could get messy. I turned toward Grace.

"Mind if I borrow that?" I asked, my eyes on her gun.

She hesitated for a moment. Then she handed over the weapon, barrel-first. While she clearly didn't trust me, Pillar City was still in (some kind of) danger. Also, there was the simple fact was that we needed each other . . . for now. As I racked the slide, I noticed that Grace's hands drifted toward the twin guns at her waistline. Fair enough.

"Consider yourself hired," I muttered, Glock in my left hand. "But there's one condition."

"What's that?" SpineSnapper eagerly asked.

"You say you're bulletproof, right?"

"Uh-huh."

"Mind if I shoot you in head?" I grinned. "Just to be sure your augmentation's good enough?"

The dumbass hesitated for a moment, which annoyed me. The fucker was almost too dumb for logic (and Harlot's power) to work on him.

"I mean you are bulletproof, right?"

"Yeah. I guess I am . . ." SpineSnapper paused. "Oh! I get it! Yeah-yeah! Shoot me."

He gave me a trusting smile, folded his arms, and assumed a solid stance. I gripped the Glock with both hands, took careful aim, and then fired one shot. The bullet went clean through his left eye, exited the back of his head, and painted the wall behind him with fresh chunks of his useless brain.

SpineSnapper IV's shocked, lifeless body fell backwards and landed hard on the old carpet with a heavy thud. I turned toward Grace, who looked just as surprised as the corpse on the floor.

"You know what?" I asked, lowering the gun. "This crime fighting thing's starting to grow on me."

CHAPTER ELEVEN

"So much for bulletproof skin," Grace gawked as I returned her gun.

"He must've bought the cheap stuff," I pretended to ponder.

Grace gave me a suspicious glance as she slipped the Glock back into its left shoulder holster.

"Do we really need all that?" I asked with a nod toward her six bags.

Grace calculated for a moment and then nodded.

"Where are you parked?" I sighed.

"Black BMW," Grace replied as she fished out her keys. "It's just a few rows in."

She tossed them my way. I pocketed the keys while Grace retrieved her Uzi. I gently grabbed her right arm as she started for the shattered doorway.

"Wait in the bathroom until I call you," I told her.

"Why?"

"It's the most secure part of this shitty room."

"Now who's being paranoid?" Grace mocked. "SpineSnapper came in here alone, Cly. There's no one else out there."

"Oh really?" I smirked. "Then how'd that idiot track you down?"

Grace started to reply . . . and then closed her mouth. The psi-hacker's face hardened as she stared beyond the doorway and into the innocent-looking night beyond.

"You're right," Grace confirmed as she pointed at SpineSnapper. "There's encrypted radio traffic nearby . . . and three different bugs embedded in his costume. Jamming them now."

"How many hostiles?"

"I can't tell," she replied with a hint of surprise in her tone. "Whoever's out there has some nice code.

Buy me some time and I'll crack into their radio chatter."

"Don't bother. I'll just go out and say hello for you."

"At least take a gun," Grace urged.

"Nah," I shook my head. "Just stay put. If I'm not back in five minutes, I'm dead."

Not thrilled about my odds, Grace went into the bathroom and closed the door. I unzipped one of the duffel bags. Inside were assorted tools and some circuit boards. She must've needed this shit to breach Hallett's lair. Her "friends" (Mitch and Seth) were probably tech experts of some kind. I wondered if her plan could work without their talents.

Zipping up the bag, I restored the metalformer/shapeshifter combo. I easily picked up all six bags, stepped around SpineSnapper's corpse, and headed outside. I heard sounds of wild sex as I passed Room #203. While I'm sure plenty of the motel's guests heard my gunshot, I doubted any of them cared (much less called the police). No one wanted flashing sirens around here.

The instant I stepped into the open, I felt watchful eyes again. Maintaining the faux metalform was starting to strain me. Much like holding an uncomfortable yoga position, I knew I couldn't keep it up for more than a few more minutes (if that). I quickened my pace.

Grace's BMW was parked close enough to easily spot. I headed downstairs, walked through the parking lot, and popped the trunk. With the bags safely inside, I slammed it shut. Taking a few steps toward the motel, I looked around and saw nothing but parked vehicles.

"C'mon guys! Don't be shy!" I yelled out with a mocking smile. "If you're after Grace, then you've gotta play with me first! Step right up and –"

Something sharp hit me right between the eyes.

I was already diving to my right as more projectiles whizzed out of the darkness. Some I dodged. Others I didn't. I rolled sideways and came up in a low crouch. My face and torso stung. A large, black shuriken was half-embedded in my titanium nose. I looked down and saw four more stuck in my chest. Angry (and a little scared), I rose and looked around. While I saw no hint of the threat, the six-pointed throwing stars were a dead giveaway.

Grace was being stalked by ninja.

These days, there were more ninja clans than brands of shampoo. Some killed. Others stole. One or two even did security work. Over the years, I've made it a point to track down the more dangerous ninja clans and bounce freelance work their way. The idea was that, with me as a valued customer, they'd be less inclined to accept contracts on my life. Judging from the quality of the hyper-alloy shuriken, I was dealing with one of those clans right now.

Unable to see my attackers, I quickly ripped the projectiles from my chest. As much as I'd love to fight my way out of this, talking would have to win the day. If this turned into a full-on fight, Grace might end up dead. Without her, whatever was threatening the city might come to pass.

I ripped the shuriken from my face and dropped it to the asphalt. One moment, I stood alone in the darkened parking lot. The next I was surrounded. I counted eighteen: all apparent humans. They wore traditional black ninja garb but with a vertical crimson stripe over the heart. The stripe signified the Crimson Blade Clan. They mainly worked Central and South America, coming stateside only when the money was right.

They liked to mix the latest tech with old-school ninja practices.

In my fixer days, I hired them—a lot.

With my luck, they already knew about my diminished status and the price on my head. Without a minor miracle, these fucks would kill me and snatch Grace on the way out. After all, the two of us were worth a combined $60 million. I put that troublesome thought out of my mind and sized up my would-be killers.

They were all male. Short and wiry, they raised their assorted weapons and moved in on me without a sound or hint of fear. I kicked on Harlot's power again. The strain was really getting to me now. Normally, I could wield multiple powers with ease, but my slow-failing augments weren't what they used to be.

"Who speaks for you?!" I yelled.

"I do," a faint whisper replied from the darkness. His Japanese accent was very pronounced. It seemed to come from everywhere at once. The voice was a bit on the elderly side. When he spoke, his subordinates paused their advance—for now.

"Who are you?" I asked in fluent Japanese.

"The Crimson Blade abandon our names," the voice replied in his native tongue. "Surrender the woman, Mr. Cly. Do it quickly and we will spare your life—for tonight, anyway. Call it a token of respect for our past association."

"Is this bounty time-sensitive?"

"No," came the reply.

"Then kidnap her tomorrow!" I complained. "Grace is here on business. There's a significant threat to the city. When it's over, she's all yours."

That last part may or may not have been a lie. But it was logical.

"Why should we care?"

"You mean, aside from the fact that you might die too?" I chuckled. "This city's full of potential clients.

Clients who sometimes hire you to hunt down hard targets in other continents. If Pillar City burns, you'd lose millions."

My argument was logical and backed by the power of psychic suggestion. It should have worked. I looked around at the ninja for any clue that Harlot's power had swayed them. They stood as still as statues.

"Kill him," the voice harshly whispered.

They would have fucking psi-shields!

I cut off Harlot's power as a well-thrown dagger whistled toward my left ear. I ducked under it and frowned as a chain wrapped around my neck from behind. My right hand grabbed it and yanked hard with my enhanced strength. Its wielder was pulled off his feet and flew past me—right through the windshield of a red '98 Porsche.

I slipped the chain from around my neck and dropped it. Four ninja came at me from the right with swords at the ready. Sparks flew as my armored arms blocked (most of) their strikes. More cuts appeared on me, though. While they felt minor now, I'd bleed out fast if I dropped the metalform.

If millions of lives—including my own—weren't at stake, I'd have turned into a metal cheetah and bolted. Instead, I grabbed the nearest ninja by the tunic and head butted him. The other three sidestepped his flying corpse and rushed in. I parried their strikes and then I grabbed two more ninja by their throats. I crushed their windpipes, dropped their corpses, and went after the last one.

Sparks flew as he slashed me across the chest. I ignored the cut, grabbed the back of his head, and then slammed his face through the hood of a beige Volvo. The poor ninja moaned before I threw him at a distant Coke machine. I missed it by over a foot . . . but he hit the wall (next to it) just fine –

And that's when the metalform failed.

Every power I rip stayed with me for about four hours. After that, they abruptly faded away. This time, the metalform prematurely expired.

Extreme pain hit me as I started to bleed all over. A feeling of sudden delirium was an added surprise. Off-balance, I dropped to my knees. Two ninja swords were within easy reach. I grabbed them with shaking, bloody hands. Then I kicked on SpineSnapper's powers, just to stay conscious. I used the faceshifter power to make my skin self-close around my many, many cuts. The dizziness quickly faded.

The pajama-wearing bitches backed off, surprised that I hadn't died. I stood up and glared them down, ready for round-fucking-two. After a moment's hesitation, they came at me. I twisted away from a lightning-fast spear thrust to my balls. The sneaky owner of said spear got himself punted across the parking lot.

Then I parried a sword swing to my throat with my new blades. I parried so hard that the attacker lost his weapon. The ninja tried to fall back but I stepped in too fast and slashed a bloody "X" through his masked face.

Another ninja darted around and tried to blindside me from the left. His blade lashed out at my eyes. I parried with my left sword and gutted him with my right. As I pulled the blade from the corpse, a hard kick slammed into the small of my back. Even with my enhanced strength, it was enough to knock me off-balance: right into a trio of incoming shuriken.

They slammed into my chest and stuck there. Blood trickled from the wounds, which hurt like hell this time. SpineSnapper's skin was a poor replacement for the metalform. The ninja (who sucker kicked me) wrapped a garrote around my neck from behind. I didn't bother to block the hardened wire. Instead, I spun to my right and sliced both swords through his legs. He screamed and clutched at the cyberstumps. So that's how he kicked so hard, eh? I drove both swords through his lungs and left them there for a moment.

I sighed at my shredded street clothes as I pulled out the shuriken. Then I closed my augmented skin over those wounds and the garrote, which was still half-embedded in my neck. I ignored the discomfort, retrieved my swords, and did a quick head count. Nine dead. Nine left.

Hot damn! I was winning!

The remaining ninja looked a bit intimidated, but they didn't have the good sense to run away either.

I barely managed to sidestep a handful of black powder, which was thrown at me by the nearest ninja. The stuff hovered in the air, began to hiss, and then slowly drifted down to the asphalt. Curious as to what it did, I chopped that ninja's left leg off. He hit the ground in shrieking pain as the falling powder went acidic on his ass.

Unfortunately, some of the stuff had gotten on my left sword. Surprised that the hardened alloy was dissolving, I flung the weapon through another ninja's stomach. As the pair of acid-burned ninja continued to scream, I assumed a two-handed fighting stance with my remaining blade held high.

Two more ninja descended from different angles. The one on the left meant to drive his sword through my face. The one on the right wanted to disembowel me. Instead of facing either attacker, I threw myself backwards—right into the (third) ninja, who had almost crept up behind me.

I didn't know for certain that he was there. It was merely an assumption because that's how ninja fought. I crashed into him hard and down we went. I back rolled over the dazed fucker, rose to one knee, and then stabbed him through the heart.

The second ninja rushed in with a hiss of rage. I hopped to my feet, parried his gut thrust, and then nailed him with a wicked left haymaker. The ninja's corpse sailed through the air until it left a large dent in the driver's side door of a red Taurus. The first ninja scored a minor cut on my right shoulder before I sliced his throat open and watched him die.

"What a waste of good talent," I muttered as I spun toward another ninja.

Armed with a pair of swords, he angrily rushed me with a blur of feints, slashes, and thrusts. I dodged, parried, and counterattacked as best I could. This ninja was way better than me, though. Worse, most of his blows struck home. Without the hardened skin, I would've been a very messy jigsaw puzzle by now. Bothered by the cuts, I skipped backwards, until I backed into the rear bumper of Grace's BMW.

The ninja moved with me and his pals gave us room to dance.

I picked my split-second and tried a hard, wide parry. But instead of blocking his swords, I blocked his arms . . . with the sharp edge of my sword. Screaming in wretched agony, the ninja fell to his knees and gawked at his severed forearms. Then he glared up at me until my back swing took his head off.

"And then there were three," I grinned as I assumed a low-guard stance and flicked some blood off my blade.

Covered in cuts, I was ready for more. With SpineSnapper's endurance, I wasn't even breathing hard. The last three ninja slowly advanced together, all eager to avenge their fallen. I paused to rip the garrote out of my neck and close up my newest wounds.

Then I stepped forward—

—and the dizziness hit me again. This time, however, it didn't go away. Shit! They had laced their weapons with some kind of tranquilizing agent (probably to bring Grace down alive). With me, their strategy was to nail me with drug-laced weapons until I dropped. It was a sneaky, gradual way to deal with hard-to-kill types.

They were about to win. I had taken too many cuts. A blackout was coming on (the type I wouldn't wake up from). I stood stock-still and gave them a feral grin, like I still had plenty of fight left in me.

"Enough!" The old man angrily shouted—in English—from behind me.

If I moved, I'd probably fall down. Another half-minute and I'd drop anyway. Had to kill these bastards fast. Give Grace half a chance to run.

"You are full of surprises, Mr. Cly," the man said . . . as another forty ninja stepped out of the darkness and surrounded me.

Fuck.

So much for holding my own. Some of the newest ninja were supers, which was the only silver lining. If one of them came too close to me, I had a chance.

"You're a bit rusty, Mr. Cly—but still formidable," said the ninja master. "Where did you learn to fight like that?"

"Catholic school," I joked with a trembling smile as the other ninja began to cautiously close in.

The old ninja chuckled.

"In another life, you could've been one of us."

"Nah," I fiercely blinked. "I wouldn't bite the hand that fed me."

"Bring me his heart," the lead ninja commanded.

"Hi guys!" Grace's voice called from above.

The ninja stopped in their tracks and turned her way. Grace leaned over the motel balcony, just outside of Room #204. She had the Uzi casually gripped in both hands with a cocky grin on her face. What the hell she was up to?!

"Sorry to interrupt. But you need to be leaving now."

"Take her," the lead ninja ordered.

Five of his minions sprinted toward the balcony. I had no doubts that they were nimble enough to get to the second floor in under three seconds.

"Have it your way," Grace sighed.

A sudden, muffled explosion occurred behind me. Everyone stopped and turned. Even I had to take a look. While the effort almost dropped me, I grinned as bits of dead lead ninja rained past me.

"That was your boss's suicide implant," Grace said. "Who's next?"

No wonder she was cocky.

The ninja swapped anxious glances. The psi-hacker narrowed her eyes as the five ninja at the balcony exploded too. Well that explained why they didn't move on her before now. They were afraid that Grace might've detected their fancy tech and started blowing them up. Instead of risking an ambush, they (somehow) steered SpineSnapper here to take the psi-hacker down. Had he succeeded, the Crimson Blade would've taken her off his (dead) hands.

"Take the hint, gents," Grace threatened. "Leave. Now."

Bowstrings were pulled. Shuriken were readied. A volley of pointy things was about to rain her way but Grace defiantly stood her ground (and why not?).

"Remember boys. She's worth more alive," I suggested before I suddenly lost control of my own body.

I plopped to the asphalt, flat on my face. I couldn't move from the neck-down and I was feeling light-headed. Sleepy, even.

"Cly!" Grace shouted with surprising concern.

"I'm okay," I yelled, barely able to turn my head to the left.

No one moved for a moment.

"Okay," I yawned, "who's the second-in-command?"

"There isn't one," one of the nearest ninja replied in perfect English.

"Then you'll do," I smiled.

Seeing as this was *The Slutty Minx,* I tried not to let my lips touch the asphalt (I might end up with syphilis or something). I gave this guy a quick glance. He was packing a fancy-looking black bow with a quiver full of black metal arrows. One of those arrows was notched and aimed at Grace. I suppressed a grin as I saw that he was a shadowporter.

With a big enough shadow this guy could create a temporary teleportation tunnel of sorts. Once he stepped through, he'd fall out of the closest shadow to his destination, anywhere else in the world. If he couldn't find a large enough shadow to jump into, he was stuck. But unlike conventional teleportation, his ability couldn't be jammed.

"Um . . . would you mind turning me over? I think we can work a deal here."

The ninja glared down at me for a moment. He should've just shot me. Instead, he rudely flipped me over with his left foot, knelt on my chest, and looked up at Grace. Then he lowered his bow—until the arrow's tip was inches from my throat. Being so close to me, the clever prick figured that Grace wouldn't risk blowing him up.

"Surrender now!" The ninja shouted, his almond eyes on Grace. "Or your friend is –"

Just like that, the ninja archer died and I felt much better.

There I was, about to pass out. If that happened, all of my closed wounds would've opened up and I'd be dead in under a minute. That's why I ripped the ninja full on. My touch can take more than just powers from a superhuman. It can take life, too—but only if I'm seriously injured.

To my relief, that particular augment hadn't failed yet. The shock of my power/life rip ended him so fast that he couldn't even manage a death cry. His lifeless fingers released the arrow, which punched through the tire of a nearby pickup truck.

"Grace!" I yelled. "Light 'em up!"

Some of the ninja threw shuriken her way but she dove under them, back into the safety of Room #204. Shuriken, arrows, and someone's energy beams flashed past me as I ducked next to a parked van and beastshifted into a black jackrabbit. My ruined clothes slid off me as I dashed away from the impending kill zone. With SpineSnapper's powers still active, I didn't feel a thing as the remaining ninja exploded behind me.

CHAPTER TWELVE

I briskly walked through the charred parking lot without a stitch of clothing. Along the way, I noticed a busted fire hydrant. I didn't need a mirror to know that I was covered in blood (most of it mine). Punctured in the blast, the hydrant spewed an arc of water into the parking lot. I stepped up into the water spray and took a quick, much-needed shower. As I scrubbed bits of dead ninja out of my hair, I kept my eyes out for any other signs of trouble.

Fortunately, the denizens of the *Slutty Minx* ignored me as they fled into the city's artificial night. Some were afraid of a second round of explosions. Others had outstanding warrants and simply wanted out before the cop cars arrived. I turned off the faceshifting ability but left the SpineSnapper powers active—just in case.

Angry shouts filled the air as owners surveyed the scorched remnants of their vehicles. There was a smoking crater where Grace's BMW (and all her precious gear) used to be. I noticed a samurai-style wakizashi stuck in a half-melted engine block. Plucking out the curved 29-inch weapon, I gave it a quick once-over. In the abundant firelight, I could see that it didn't have a nick on it. Even though it didn't come with a scabbard, the hyper-alloy weapon would make a worthy souvenir.

Then I turned to size up *The Slutty Minx.* Grace had made quite a mess of the place. The shrapnel-pocked building was blackened in some parts and gore-splattered in others. The windows on this side were all blown out. Even the motel's neon sign was shattered by the blasts.

Ah well. Not my mess.

As I headed upstairs, a skinny guy ran past me (wearing only a white clown mask and a grass skirt). I chuckled at the sight, just happy to be alive. I reached #204 as Grace achingly rose to her feet and stepped out onto the balcony.

"Time to go," I said, half-relieved that she wasn't dead.

The psi-hacker was clearly unimpressed as she looked me over.

"I thought you were human," she frowned.

"Well I'm definitely not a vegetable or mineral," I replied as I brushed passed her. "You still want to get into that lair?"

The "L" word snapped her back into focus as I stepped over the late SpineSnapper's corpse.

"Yeah," Grace urgently replied.

"Then I'm coming with you. And here's my price: I get to keep whatever I want."

"Cly," she sighed. "We don't have time for this!"

As much as I wanted to use Harlot's power on her, my gut told me not to. Whatever was buzzing around in her head scared me enough. Also, I'd be amazed if The Outfitter hadn't given her some kind of psi-shield to protect her mind (and his secrets) from psychic intrusion.

Sirens blared in the distance. While *The Slutty Minx* wasn't mob-owned, its absentee owner paid solid protection money to Pillar City's finest. In return, the police rarely (if ever) came down here unless the motel management called for help. Still, the cops couldn't ignore a mess this big.

Grace didn't react to the sirens. Maybe her ears were still ringing from the explosions.

"I hear police sirens," I warned her with a raised voice. "We do this my way or you can try to flee the scene on your own . . . and die with the rest of the city."

There were more sirens. From all sides. Grace finally noticed them. A police chopper showed up, spotlight and all. That wasn't good. Typically, only a few cop cars could get here so fast. Whenever choppers showed up, SWAT wasn't far behind. With this many cops already in the vicinity, I knew it had to be for a coordinated raid.

Maybe they were after one of the motel guests. Or, more realistically, they were here for Grace. They'd bring her in for questioning. A pair of "feds" would come along and collect her with fake transfer orders.

Grace would never be seen again.

Any investigation into her disappearance would be 110% bullshit. Whichever cops spearheaded the investigation would suddenly "come into money" and head off to a tropical retirement. With the bounties on Grace's head, the idea wasn't too far-fetched. One look at Grace's nervous eyes told me that she had reached the same conclusion.

"What's it gonna be?" I pressed.

"Deal," she grumbled. "Now, how are you getting us out?"

"Hold this," I said, handing her the wakizashi.

Grace frowned as she took the weapon by its hilt. I stepped into the bathroom and grabbed the biggest white towel I could find. I flicked it a few times (to get the roaches off), dried myself off, and then wrapped it around my waist. I turned off the bathroom light and grabbed Grace by her left arm. We both could hear approaching footsteps running up from outside.

Probably the SWAT team.

"Don't lose that blade!" I barked.

I pulled her into the shadows of the bathroom as a pair of flash-bang grenades were rolled into the room.

"What are you doing –?!" Grace managed to ask, right before I dragged us into a shadow tunnel.

*   *   *

Grace screamed as we fell through utter darkness.

Shadowporting was a useful form of teleportation—but not the best. If you can envision the target (a person, thing, or place) you can come out of his/her/its shadow. To get there, a shadow tunnel needed to pass through . . . Shadow. While this plane of existence was just as real as the outside world, it ran by different rules.

Throughout the centuries, scholars and scientists argued about the mechanics of shadowporting. The one thing they agreed upon was that you shouldn't shadowport from the same vicinity more than once. Those who ignored this wisdom disappeared into Shadow and rarely reemerged.

With that in mind, I aimed my thoughts for the Hallett house.

Grace clamped onto me like a scared child. Though I knew it would only take seconds, it felt like minutes. Then we abruptly slid out of a half-closed basement closet, skidded a few feet across a concrete floor, and then slammed into a wood-paneled wall. I took the brunt of the impact, which was eased by SpineSnapper's armored skin.

There was movement behind us. We both looked up and realized that we weren't alone. Grace started to raise her Uzi.

"Hold fire!" I shouted as I grabbed her gun arm.

Unable to get a clean shot, Grace gave me a dubious look. Then she reluctantly lowered her weapon, which was a good thing. Frankly, she had almost gotten us killed.

"Report," I ordered with a relieved grin.

"The site's secured," Dirtnap replied with a thick Georgia twang.

At fifty-one, Johnny Ferguson, a.k.a. Dirtnap, was one of my best ex-contractors. Tall and lean, the hard-faced super was sporting a graying brown mustache and thinning hair. He wore black jeans, a white mock turtleneck, and a layer of sweat. He was in his black socks, which meant that we had interrupted a training session.

Dirtnap was arguably one of the best bounty hunters who ever lived. Put him on someone's trail and he was relentless. Before 9/11, he was a bit overstressed. His frisky wife had just pushed out baby number six. To feed them, he chased all manner of violent scumbags across the country.

Then the Towers fell and thousands died—one of them being his baby sister.

I took advantage of Dirtnap's rage and convinced him to work for me. At first, he ran down Islamic terror cells. Whenever things were slow, I tasked him with the "honest" jobs (protection gigs, rescue ops, training, etc.). Over the years, I kept him in diaper/tuition money. He got me results and made me seem like less of a "scumbag temp service" to prospective clients. While Dirtnap didn't invite me to Thanksgiving dinner, we had mutual respect.

What most folks didn't know about Dirtnap was that he was a super. Tired of dodging bullets, he bought some phasing augments last year. He could now walk through walls, people, and most other types of matter. Frankly, he didn't need super powers. Next to Pinpoint, Dirtnap was my best shooter. He was smart, experienced, and preferred a dirty fight to a clean one. And when the shit came down, he'd break out Junior.

Junior was the name of his beloved hand cannon, which fired micro-artillery shells. Each of his normal-looking bullets could blow the door off a pickup truck. The custom-made rectangular weapon had recoil vents along both sides, a 30-round mag in the grip, and a curved filleting blade under the barrel. The hyper-alloy blade's tip extended three inches beyond the barrel, like an underside cleaver/bayonet.

The gun itself was about a foot long, six inches high, and four inches wide. His hip holster had to be metallic to safely hold such a weapon. Dirtnap bragged that Junior was always within reach (even when he was banging his wife). Right now, Junior was gripped loosely in Dirtnap's lowered right hand. If Grace even twitched wrong, he'd smear her *through* the nearest wall. I looked around the damp, empty basement. Illuminated by ceiling panels, it was large enough to spar in or hold a quaint little house party.

"We come at a bad time?" I asked.

"Naw," Dirtnap replied with a curious gleam in his eye. "Just having a quick review."

"What happened to your suit?" Forecast asked as she lowered her MP5 submachine gun and stepped up next to Dirtnap.

"Don't ask," I grinned in reply.

Her freckled, innocent face made me forget my troubles for a moment. Forecast was the child I'd never have. The simple truth was that kids were vulnerabilities with dimples: nothing more. As a fixer, I've exploited that weakness more times than I could count.

But Forecast was a complication, a weakness, and the light of my life.

She kept her black hair cut short, with deep green eyes that reminded me of her mother's way too often. Sweaty and toned, the kid wore a beige pair of cargo paints and a red t-shirt. Her boobs were still tiny but her ass was turning into quite the distracting plum. At the tender age of fifteen, more and more males were paying attention to her.

While I wished I could act like an overprotective father, doing so would only get her killed. It only seemed like yesterday when I was teaching Forecast how to tie her shoes. Now, I was worried about what I'd do to the first asshole that broke her heart.

"I hope you were holding your own, kid."

"Of course," Forecast proudly replied.

"How'd you get here?" Dirtnap asked.

Grace looked my way, curious as well.

"I don't remember," I blatantly lied as I secured my towel and stood up. "And don't change the subject. Why hasn't Forecast kicked your ass by now?"

"I was just about to tap out when you two showed up," Dirtnap joked, eyes locked on Grace.

The ex-cop saw coiled death behind Dirtnap's polite demeanor. She sighed before dropping both the Uzi and the wakizashi. He gave her a slight nod and eased his posture—a bit. After all, Grace wore four other guns. I gallantly held out my right hand, which Grace accepted. I pulled her to her feet.

"Grace," I said, running a quick introduction, "this is Dirtnap and Forecast."

Grace nodded.

Forecast waved while Dirtnap nodded back.

"Got any clothes around here?"

"That'll fit you?" Dirtnap asked, sizing up my gut and love handles. "No."

"I could check upstairs," Forecast offered.

"Thanks," I replied.

Forecast handed me her submachine gun like it was a toy and headed upstairs.

The mere sight of her reminded me of how cruel Fate can be. I was friends with her mom, Becka Falsham. A goodie-two-shoes type, she was the day to my night. Unfortunately, she was also married. Her husband, Tom, was her soul mate and all-around good guy. They were happy together when I met them at an airport in Zaire, back in '96. Both of them were doctors bouncing through the African continent, looking to save lives and see exotic lands. I was posing as a freelance merc, pretending to make a name for myself.

I loved Becka from the moment I saw her.

Only discipline—and the fact that she loved Tom— kept me from seducing her. I settled for becoming friends with the happy couple. We swapped letters, photos, and local souvenirs. I selfishly hoped that their marriage would collapse under the stress of "do-goodery" in the Third World. Instead, about a year later, Becka called to tell me she was pregnant. In their seventh year of marriage, they were still in Africa and never happier.

I begged them to head stateside until the baby was safely born. Unfortunately, they were needed in Somalia. I canceled a few jobs and made my way there during the eighth month of her pregnancy. They knew I was coming. Aside from my spare mags and plastique, I had packed diapers, champagne, earplugs, and cigars. During quick sat phone calls, we playfully argued about baby names . . .

By the time I arrived, Becka and Tom were dead.

Their relief convoy was en route to save some injured dipshits when bandits ambushed it. Tom died shielding his wife from AK-47 fire . . . not that it saved her. One of the other doctors (a healer) managed to save the baby. I claimed the infant and left her someplace safe.

Then I personally dealt with the bandits.

And their wives.

And their kids.

And anyone else unlucky enough to get in my fucking way.

I might've kept on killing if not for the child. I took her back to the U.S., along with her parents' remains. During an airport layover, I named the baby Lia. Tom was raised in foster homes and had no known relatives. Becka had parents in Peoria, who happily took her in and raised her. I visited as discreetly as possible (especially when I became a fixer).

Lia's grandparents knew I was a shady bastard but they didn't object to the money I sent their way each month. They even named me her godfather, which made sense in a messed-up way. Still, Lia might've had a normal life had her power not manifested when she was ten.

Normal humans having a superhuman child was rare. Lia turned out to be a precog (a coveted ability). The messed-up thing was that Lia didn't even realize it at first. Most precogs have visions of the future—theirs and/or someone else's.

In Lia's case, however, anyone she touched had visions of their futures, which she herself couldn't see. Back then, Lia didn't know how to turn off her gift. Thus, everyone she touched ended up with visions of their own futures—ranging anywhere from minutes to decades.

Word spread, of course.

Her grandparents (idiots) didn't tell me until after the second kidnapping attempt. By then, I had plenty of contractors. We rescued Lia and made her kidnappers extinct. I'm sure her parents would've wanted Lia to live a normal life. I wanted her to live a safe one.

That's why I took her in.

Lia lived with some of my telepath contractors at first. They taught her how to use (and control) her powers. They also kept her safe when I wasn't around. I saw to it that she was taught how to defend herself and survive all kinds of hairy situations. By her twelfth birthday, Lia picked her call sign and went to work for me.

Naturally, I never let Forecast into the field. But once in a while, especially when planning a hairy op, she came in handy. I would sit the contractors down with a telepath. They'd wear hoods, to protect Forecast's identity. Then she'd touch the contractors, one-by-one. The telepath would scan their minds, see their visions, and relay them to me. Then we'd adjust our plans.

Forecast's visions were never vague or wrong. Left unchanged, her visions came to pass without exception. If a future operation was destined to go off without a hitch, I'd have the visions wiped from the contractors' minds. That way, their actions couldn't be swayed by what they saw. Should the visions warn us of an impending clusterfuck, we'd make adjustments.

The kid's power came with limitations though. In spite of their best efforts, my telepaths could never teach Forecast how to see her own future. She also couldn't see the visions of anyone she touched. Nor could she ever give more than one vision per day to the same person. In spite of these odd limitations, Forecast was one of my best operatives.

Since her mind was too strong to be psi-trained, Forecast had to learn everything the old-fashioned way. Luckily, she was just as smart and determined as her mom. She studied and trained eight hours a day, seven days a week.

Her ties to me were a well-kept secret among a handful of my contractors (like Dirtnap) who were paid extra to keep it that way. Now that I was no longer a fixer, I had to expect one/more of them to sell me out. Maybe that's why Dirtnap brought her here tonight, as a precaution. So much shit was going on with me that I had completely forgotten about my own goddaughter's well being. That was a true sign that my inner asshole was still alive and strong.

Maybe it was better that I never had kids of my own.

"I owe you," I told Dirtnap.

The gunslinger nodded with a brief glance toward the stairs.

"I was about to get her out of town," he shrugged. "But the kid didn't want to leave without knowing you were all right. Then I remembered that Gratte put some people on this old house a few days ago. Figured that we'd lend a hand, lie low, and wait for you to turn up."

Grace's face perked up at the mention of Gratte's name.

"This is the lair?" Grace frowned.

Dirtnap glanced my way with sudden understanding (and worry) in his eyes. Well-equipped lairs attracted all kinds of trouble. He picked his gun belt off the floor.

"We should go," Dirtnap urged as he holstered Junior.

"Who else is here?" I pressed.

Dirtnap began to strap the holster against his right hip.

"Ray and Teke," he replied. "They're in the backyard."

"Where's Gratte?" Grace asked.

Dirtnap glanced at her. Then he looked my way, silently asking me if she was okay to talk around. I nodded.

"Not a peep since Thursday," he answered, a bit worried. "I was about to see if any of your 'ex-employees' wanted to form a posse and track him down."

Dirtnap walked over to his black cowboy boots and put them back on. I paused and weighed the most likely ·

scenarios. Having known Gratte for years, three came to mind.

"He's either in hiding, selling me out, or being tortured," I assessed. "Either way, I doubt even you could find him."

"We'll see about that," Dirtnap scoffed as he checked the gun belt to make sure it was secure.

"Where's the lair?" Grace insistently asked.

"This way," I sighed, heading for the stairs with the MP5 in my hands.

Grace picked up the Uzi as she followed. Dirtnap calmly retrieved the wakizashi and took up the rear.

"Why do you care about a lair, Cly?" Dirtnap asked. "I thought you were out of the game."

I was surprised that Dirtnap didn't know about the Community Service verdict. I stopped at the foot of the stairway.

"What've you heard?"

"That you had Seamus O'Flernan put down," he shrugged. "And that you sold us out to save your own neck."

"Basically," I admitted. "I wasn't in the mood for all-out war. This town's worth a lot of money and it'd be a shame to burn it to the ground over a misunderstanding."

"Why not?" Dirtnap sneered. "We'd have backed you up."

Dirtnap hated Pillar City and the mobs that ruled it. The idea of trading lead with them appealed to his sense of honor. Had he known the angles though, the country boy would've agreed with me. All four mobs outgunned us. My connections (many of whom also took bribes from the mobs) wouldn't side with me in a messy, protracted war.

Also, any of my contractors might've sold me out if offered enough money/coercion (even Dirtnap). Harlot could "suggest" that he kill me. Or Ronns could just snatch his family.

"My beef was with Seamus," I patiently explained. "Escalating it wasn't worth the grief."

Dirtnap gave me a sympathetic sigh.

"Well, you're gonna love this part," Dirtnap said as he walked past us. "Everyone you brought in on that extraction op's dead—except for Pinpoint and Anywhere. They're both MIA."

I took the news in stride as I turned and followed him up the stairs.

"Who aced them?"

"The Irish. They brought in a bunch of heavy-hitter types—probably to make you dead."

"What else?" I pressed.

"Your ex-employees—myself included—all got texts from the local mobs. They told us to either sign up with them or stay out of Pillar City. My guess is that violators will get gunned down with extreme glee. We've got 24 hours to decide."

"I took the Community Service option," I told him.

The gunslinger's eyes narrowed as he stopped and sized me up.

"You're gonna be a crime fighter?!" Dirtnap asked with a mocking smile.

"He might pull it off," Grace grudgingly admitted, having seen me fight.

"Maybe with some super powers and a few years' worth of gym time!" Dirtnap chuckled. "You won't last a day, Cly. Why didn't you bang it out?"

"Because I couldn't win," I irritably snapped. "Me against all four mobs? At once? With no advanced planning or element of surprise? I wouldn't win and you know it."

Dirtnap shook his head but gave up the argument— for now. Maybe he had a point about me standing my ground. But that's the hard lesson about being a fixer in a large pond; if you have to stand your ground, you've already lost.

CHAPTER THIRTEEN

Dirtnap led Grace and me through an unfurnished kitchen and out the back door. The house's rear floodlights were on, making everything easy to see. This quiet street was lined with old homes, set back-to-back, except for this one.

The house behind Hallett's had been torn down long ago. The lot was artfully merged into the backyard, which more than doubled its length. The driveway was extended and the two-car garage was moved back. Between the house and the garage was a large, ovular swimming pool, which had been built over this supposed lair.

White-lined, emptied, and full of cracks, the pool had seen better days. It was surrounded by Gratte's gear, most of which was covered by blue tarps. The rest of the yard was littered with discarded beer cans and used condoms. The backyard, with its fancy pool, was ideal for a poor man's skate park and late-night parties. I'll bet the neighborhood kids enjoyed some wild "sexcapades" back here.

"Sound off," I said.

"Since you asked nicely," Ray Paldo replied from above.

Startled, Grace spun and started to raise the Uzi . . . only to freeze in her tracks. She had good reason. I couldn't make out the gun in Ray's right hand but it came with a green laser sight, which was already centered on Grace's forehead. Knowing Ray, it was probably his suppressor-capped MK23 pistol. Loaded with .45 ACP rounds, Ray could've blown her head off without waking the neighbors.

Another one of my former contractors, Ray wore his brown hair short, with bright gray eyes and a farmer's tan. At 5'11", the twenty year-old had a lean build and boyishly-handsome face. Tonight, he wore a gray repairman's uniform and matching cap.

"What happened to your clothes?" Ray asked with a curious smile.

"Oh, I just finished filming a low-budget porno and thought I'd go for a swim," I joked as I set the MP5 on the porch steps.

"Quit showin' off and fall in!" Dirtnap growled.

Ray nodded then nimbly rolled off the roof. He holstered his sidearm in mid-fall and landed right in front of me. His MK23 hung from a low holster on his right hip. On his back was a Steyr AUG carbine with a low-light scope. A clear plastic ear bud ran down from his left ear and into his uniform's collar.

"Nice reflexes, Grace," Ray said with a charming smile.

"How'd you know my name?" Grace suspiciously asked.

"Your wardrobe's a dead giveaway," he replied with a nod toward her five visible weapons and *corporate chic* attire.

"Sorry. I'm getting a bit paranoid these days," Grace replied with an embarrassed smile.

"No apologies needed," Ray said as he held out a hand. "Ray Paldo. Pleasure to meet you."

As they shook hands, I searched for Teke but didn't see him.

"Status?" I evenly asked.

"Aside from a few squirrels, a mean-looking cat, and your lady friend's Uzi, no threats to report," Ray replied. "We expecting trouble?"

"Yeah," I answered.

"Good," he said before leaning in to whisper, "I was getting bored."

Even though Ray was a smartass, I was glad to have him here.

A third-generation speedster, Ray Paldo was born to a pair of honest-to-God super heroes who expected him to go into the family business. As he grew up, they taught him everything they knew about crime fighting. When he turned eighteen, they had planned to unleash him on the criminal underworld, under the call sign of "Kid Nimble."

Too bad his genes had other ideas.

When he was fifteen, Ray woke up one morning and could barely run a thirty-second mile. He could still count falling rain drops, hit like a jackhammer, and dodge automatic fire for hours at a time. He just couldn't run faster than quarter-MACH. If Ray ended up a hero, he might've done just fine—especially if he had to rely on his super-fast wits.

Lucky for us crooks, his parents were assholes.

Horrified at the thought of him being inferior, they sent Ray to the best specialists and healers they could find. None of them could heal the lad because he wasn't (technically) sick. His mutation was naturally-occurring and could only be reversed by a very radical form of gene therapy. They were warned that the process came with potentially-dangerous side effects. To Ray's disgust, his parents signed him up right then and there.

Ray didn't just leave home—he became a crook. His intent wasn't to rebel against his parents (who eventually disowned him). He simply saw a brighter future in crime than in crime fighting. As his parents were now dead and he wasn't, I'd say he was right. By the time he turned eighteen, Ray Paldo was wanted in thirteen countries and had become a rising star in the criminal world. Naturally, I recruited him.

That was two years ago.

Since then, he's been one of my best field assets.

"Teke!" Dirtnap impatiently looked around. "Front and center!"

The Georgia gunslinger felt a tug at the back of his shirt and half-turned to find Teke waiting behind him. With his flair for mental illusions, the little bastard might've been standing there the whole time. Grace frowned with disapproval because she thought he was a mere child. In reality, Teke was actually 61 years old.

Due to some odd genetic disorder, he stopped growing (and aging) when he was ten. The old man was six when his psychic powers began to manifest. His abilities developed enough to get him into the Army at twenty-one, where he worked military intelligence for most of his career. As a combat telepath, Teke had seen more wars and run more black ops than even me. I should know because he recruited and psi-trained me. Had he not been framed for high treason, Colonel Roman A. Koss would've been enjoying his retirement on a beach somewhere.

Instead, he came to work for me—with a new face and ethnicity. These days, I only gave Teke lightweight ops (like watching over an abandoned lair). Tonight, he wore blue jeans, black Converse high-tops, and an olive-colored sweater. Skinny, black, and adorable, his hair was cut short. His brown eyes sized up Grace with apparent mistrust. He must've sensed her psychic instability –

Wait a second. I glanced over at Ray.

"What's with the ear bud?" I asked him.

"I'm tapped into the police band," he evenly replied. "You've had quite a night, Mr. Cly."

I took a deep breath.

"How bad?" I asked.

Ray gave me an intrigued smile.

"You're wanted for a 'motel bombing' and a string of murders—starting with Seamus O'Flernan and ending with a muscular John Doe with really bad breath."

I muttered some choice profanities as Grace stifled her laughter in the background.

"Who else did I allegedly kill?" I asked.

"About fifty O'Flernan mobsters, three feds, and something about ninjas –"

"Whoa! Stop!" I got in his face. "Did you say 'three feds'?"

"Yeah. At the *Versantio Hotel*," Ray replied. "Three undercover FBI agents were found dead in a rooftop restaurant."

Undercover my ass!

I sighed and looked up at the cold night sky. The feds labeled those three agents "undercover" to avoid a scandal. It was the only way they could explain three (dirty) feds hanging around Seamus O'Flernan— especially with Mockre dying in a coffin one floor below them.

I was the logical patsy.

Still, this was some impressive spin control. My guess was that the O'Flernans had a hand in setting me up. When this was over, Harlan Ronns would have an appointment with a shallow-fucking grave.

"Get me some clothes," I scowled. "We've got work to do."

"Way ahead of ya'," Teke assured me. "Once the police broke into your loft, Ray slipped in and grabbed a few–"

"My loft?!" I cut him off. "They busted into my place?"

"Yeah," Teke nodded. "About two hours ago."

Pillar City cops had notoriously sticky fingers and very short memories. I paid them monthly to leave me and mine alone. They wouldn't have come near my home unless they knew about my Community Service. Aside from my decent art collection, I'm sure they'd find all three of my hidden safes, each with $10 million in cash. I wonder if a third of that money would ever make it to the Evidence Room.

"Clothes!" I growled.

Teke glanced at the distant garage and narrowed his eyes. The door opened, courtesy of his telekinesis. Out floated a fully packed go-bag and one of my black suits. I kept the beige canvas go-bag in my loft for shitty days like this. The black, three-piece suit (while just a regular Armani) looked better on me than a damned towel.

Without further ado, I changed clothes. As I did, everyone wisely gave me some fucking space. I used the quiet interlude to calm down and return my mind to the job at hand. The mobs, police, and the rest of my enemies would have to wait.

I rolled up my white shirt's sleeves and then put on my Platinum Rolex. I secured a pair of shoulder-holstered Walther PPX's to my torso. Then I pulled a wad of c-notes. I stuffed it into my suit jacket.

"Where's your armor?" Dirtnap asked as he jammed the wakizashi into the lawn.

"It's a pile of ashes," I muttered as I pulled a clean burner phone from the go-bag.

"Who slagged it?" Teke asked with a bothered frown.

He had seen my armor take a lot of abuse over the years. The thought of it getting destroyed rightfully worried him.

"Spetrovich," I replied as I tucked the phone into my suit jacket.

"Want him dead?" Ray half-seriously offered. "It'll be our little secret."

"Don't tempt me."

Forecast frowned as she stepped out to find me in a fancy new suit. She had scrounged up a large gray t-shirt, yellow flip-flops, and pair of burgundy sweat pants.

"Thanks anyway," I told her with a guilty smile as I checked my guns.

Forecast sighed, dropped the clothes on the porch, and then picked up the MP5 as she walked over and joined us.

"What exactly did you get yourself into this time?" Teke asked, eyeing me like I was a flat-out idiot.

"Just see for yourself!" I snapped, tired of answering tons of fucking questions.

Teke shrugged and then read my mind. I let him in solely due to decades of hard-earned trust on his part. Teke narrowed his eyes as he read my memories of the last few hours. His initial reaction was amazement . . . followed by a satisfied smile.

"Not bad, Cly," he remarked. "Not bad at all."

"Wow! A compliment?" I teased with a wry grin. "What was your favorite part?"

"Fleecing Spetrovich, of course!" He chuckled. "Too bad you couldn't kill Harlot right then and there."

"Lemme see!" Forecast mildly whined.

I could tell that the others were equally curious.

"You only get the PG-13 stuff, kid," Teke sternly replied.

The telepath gave Grace a look of pure loathing. Everyone—including Grace—noticed it. Oh yeah, Teke sensed her instability all right. Whatever was going on in her mind, he wanted no part of it.

"Everyone else too?" Teke frowned.

"Yeah," I nodded.

He sighed then sent an audio-visual copy of my memories to the others (minus my thoughts). When it was over, Dirtnap chuckled. Forecast regarded me with awe. Ray looked on with a hint of envy. I could practically hear the questions buzzing around in Grace's head.

At least she was smart enough not to ask them.

"Well, this might cheer you up a bit," Dirtnap smiled as he stepped up and put both of his hands through my chest.

"Not really," I smirked as I felt the tingling sensation of being phased.

He then pulled his left hand out and held it up for me to see. In his weathered palm was a white, dime-shaped device.

"The tracker bomb?" I knowingly asked him.

"Figured you might want that out before someone hit you the wrong way," Dirtnap replied as he pulled out his right hand.

The tingling sensation went away.

"Thanks," I replied as I took the bomb and handed it to Grace.

As she reluctantly took the damned thing and slipped it into a pocket, I noticed that Ray was unusually quiet.

"What?" I asked with a hint of irritation.

"Later," he replied. "After I check on a few things."

I rolled my eyes, picked up my blade, and gestured toward the pool. The others followed.

"Give me time and I might be able to track down your two missing contractors," Grace offered.

"They're better off lost," I replied, hoping that Pinpoint and Anywhere were still alive.

I stopped as something Nunez asked on *The Depravity* popped in my head.

"That woman on the rooftop with Seamus—the one posing as a server—can you ID her?"

The psi-hacker pondered the question for a moment.

"Help me out and I'll get you a name" she replied.

I grudgingly nodded, annoyed by the fact that I might owe Grace Lexia a favor or two before this was over.

"Um . . . what is this threat, exactly?" Ray asked. Grace didn't answer.

Instead, she stepped past Gratte's equipment, knelt over a tarp, and flipped it aside. Beneath it was a shallow drop into a five-foot tunnel. Grace hopped in without hesitation. We cautiously followed.

Smooth and stable, this new tunnel went all of ten feet before intersecting with the escape tunnel (which was about seven feet high and twenty feet wide). Red, baseball-sized guide lights ran along the length of the tunnel's concrete ceiling. As we entered, the lights flickered on. To our left, the tunnel ran off into the distance. A few yards to our right, a thick metal door blocked the way. It lacked markings or insignias.

"Accessing door controls," Grace announced.

The psi-hacker closed her eyes and tense seconds passed . . .

Naturally, nothing fucking happened.

"What's wrong?" Forecast asked.

"The lair's broken," I muttered. "Dirtnap, if you would?"

Dirtnap casually drew his massive sidearm and phased before slowly walking through the thick door.

"I've got eyes on him," Teke muttered.

"Well, is it a lair or not?" Forecast excitedly asked.

Teke was part-mystified, all-worried about what he saw through Dirtnap's eyes.

"This isn't just a lair," he ominously replied. "It's a Way Station."

CHAPTER FOURTEEN

Ray discreetly drew his pistol and kept an eye on our six o'clock.

"Come again?" I asked with an irritated glance at Grace.

"It's an ArgoKnight Way Station," Grace confirmed. "That's why I was so reluctant to bring you anywhere near it."

She had a point . . . seeing as I helped wipe them out last year.

The ArgoKnights were real-life super heroes who prowled the streets and soared through the clouds, fighting evil in an old school, hard-hitting way. For sixty-eight years, they saved the world from all kinds of threats to humanity. Half of the old hero groups were started and/or supported by them.

Personally, I hated the fuckers.

They took down some of my better-paying clients. Once or twice, they almost brought me down. Fortunately, like all "good" things, they came to an end.

On February 9th, 2011, they were massacred during *Clean Sweep*. It was a glorious, lucrative blitzkrieg in which every hero group in the world was simultaneously targeted by an overwhelming number of super villains and their minions. When the smoke cleared, every hero group—including the ArgoKnights—was either dead or MIA.

Ironically, I now found myself standing outside of a Way Station, hoping to steal enough shit to survive another day or three. These fully-stocked field bases were designed to provide tactical support for ArgoKnights in the field. A Way Station's AI could track their movements, provide real-time intel, and coordinate any necessary backup. The sites were well-hidden and scattered throughout the world—usually near large cities and/or habitual trouble spots.

It made sense that Pillar City would have (at least) one.

Dirtnap phased through the door and rejoined us a few seconds later, a sad look on his face.

"The door controls don't work," Dirtnap reported as he holstered Junior. "We'll have to force it open."

"How?" Grace scoffed. "That door's designed to withstand up to forty tons of –"

The vault door's frame groaned for a moment, then slid open to the left.

"You were saying?" Teke muttered.

Grace gawked at the little telepath's casual display of power.

Stale air gushed out as we entered. Some long-dormant power generator kicked in and the overhead lighting activated. Ventilation systems hummed and began to address the air quality. As the rest of us followed, I looked up. An old ArgoKnight logo was painted on the ceiling—in the form of a white chess piece with "ARGOKNIGHTS" (stenciled) around it in black lettering.

"No wonder it wasn't destroyed or looted by now," Ray replied, after taking a quick look around the room. "This Way Station was decommissioned long before *Clean Sweep*."

"Yep," Grace reverently replied. "The Outfitter mentioned it once. But he never told me the exact location."

At the center of the room was a pentagon-shaped computer server with five terminals, all of which were deactivated. In one corner of the room was a downward flight of metal stairs, which likely led to the Transport Level and its teleportation grids.

"That's why you had all those tools at *The Slutty Minx*," I said to Grace. "To make repairs."

"Yeah," she frowned. "One of my 'friends'—Mitch—was a super genius . . . and a coward too."

"I don't get it," Forecast frowned. "If they shut this place down, why didn't they take it apart?"

"Two reasons," Ray theorized. "First, it would require too much effort, time, and risk to covertly dismantle this site. Second, an old Way Station could easily be 'lost' from their official records and serve as a fallback bunker."

"How many of these 'bunkers' are out there?" Forecast asked.

"Hundreds, possibly," Ray explained. "The ArgoKnights decommissioned their Way Stations once every five years because their technology evolved too quickly. Upgrades would've been too costly and time-consuming to make, so they'd just mothball them."

He glanced around the room again.

"This one was active during the . . . early 80's, judging from the tech. I don't believe anyone's set foot in here since then."

"Can you make do with this antique?" I asked with a nod toward the terminal.

"I came prepared," Grace confidently replied as she tapped her forehead. "I've got enough software upgrades to bring the AI to current standards. The thing is, I should've been able to psi-hack into it from the outside. Right now, this place is only running on secondary power and the AI is completely down."

"So something's off-line in here and you have no idea what?"

"Yeah," she told me. "Until we fix it, the AI's just a piece of modern art."

That might be a tall order. Way Stations were typically built like an upside-down pyramid with three levels: Support, Transportation, and Medical. The lair was crammed with tons of one-of-a-kind, outdated super tech.

"How do we fix this, Ray?" I asked.

"I'd have to pop the hood and find out," he shrugged.

"Take your time," I confidently replied.

Then I turned to admire the Argoknight tech (now *my* tech). Shelves of weapons and supplies still lined the three-cornered room. Each shelf was hermetically-sealed behind hardened, transparent plastic. I couldn't wait to find out how much of this shit still worked. Whether the ArgoKnight tech was two years old or thirty-plus, it was still better than nothing.

Ray handed me his carbine and headed for the escape tunnel.

"Wait," Grace got in front of him. "No offense— but do you know what you're doing?"

Ray gave her a modest grin.

"You be the judge," he replied before zipping past her in a blur of sub-sonic speed.

Three seconds later, he was back with one of Gratte's tarps. I grinned and signaled the others to step back and let the man work. In under a minute, Ray had made over thirty round-trips. By now, all of Gratte's lightweight gear was neatly placed around the room.

"Need me to move anything heavy?" Teke offered.

"Nah," Ray shook his head. "I'm good."

Ray stretched out some kinks in his back . . . and then he became a living blur. The bastard moved so fast that he looked to be in eight places at once. We watched him tear down five control chairs, the five-person workstation, and get into the guts of the AI server—in about fourteen (maybe fifteen) seconds. The speedster abruptly paused and tossed Grace a thin white piece of plastic. At first glance, the rectangular thingee looked a bit singed.

"How clever," Ray smiled through a grime-covered face.

"What?" Grace asked.

He pointed at the damaged part.

"Someone pulled out that control chip, seared its edges, and then put it back in. Without a working chip, this whole site's useless."

"Like pulling the spark plug from a car?" Dirtnap asked.

"Basically," Ray nodded.

"Did Gratte bring a compatible spare?" I asked.

Ray chuckled and swiftly picked up three of them.

"Love him or hate him, Gratte always came prepared," he winked before reassembling the server.

Nine seconds later, the console looked good-as-new. Ray even took a split-second to polish the damned thing. Grace gave me a hopeful smile and then stared at one of the gleaming terminals.

It activated.

"Give me . . . ten minutes and the AI should be 'live' again," Grace announced.

"Nicely done," I turned to Ray. "Now clean up this mess, willya'?"

Ray gave me a playful salute and then zipped off to comply. As he buzzed around the room, I wondered who Vivian Hallett really was. Most folks would've assumed that she was an ArgoKnight. Then again, she might've been some poor civilian who moved into the wrong house. Or maybe she was just a "caretaker" for the place all along.

Each active Way Station was manned by members of the ArgoKnight Support Staff. Almost a thousand-strong, they kept the ArgoKnights' varied bases and operations running smoothly—allowing the heroes to focus more on saving the day. Most staffers were either ex-soldiers or brilliant geeks. A few were even supers themselves.

They were stupidly loyal, too. During the dark days of *Clean Sweep*, they manned their stations to the end, trying to save as many ArgoKnights as possible. Rumor was that none of them survived. When this was over, I'd have to track this Vivian Hallett down—just out of curiosity.

Ray zipped back into the room while Grace sat down at the terminal and put her Uzi next to it.

"Anything else?" Ray offered.

"Get back on overwatch," I replied as I handed his carbine back to him. "Thanks for coming through."

"It's what you *pay* me for," the speedster hinted as he slung the Steyr over his back. "One more thing— whatever you're up to next, I want in."

"You sure about that?" Dirtnap asked, echoing my thoughts.

Ray nodded as he gave Grace a parting wave.

"Sure I'm sure! I actually took a whole quarter-second to think it over," he grinned before zipping out of the room.

When he left, Teke turned toward the tunnel entrance and telekinetically closed the door. Dirtnap looked up at the ArgoKnight logo with clear nostalgia and regret.

"They were the best of the best," he said.

I bit back an insult because I respected Dirtnap. When *Clean Sweep* broke, he wanted to help the heroes. I (barely) managed to talk him out of it. In retrospect, I saved his life. Most of the folks who stepped in to help ended up dead.

Dirtnap didn't want to admit that the ArgoKnights were doomed for one simple reason: they let their enemies live. Imagine locking away all kinds of super villains for sixty-eight fucking years. They had so many goddamned enemies—from ruthless masterminds to alien warlords to dumbassed minions—that *Clean Sweep* was destined to occur.

The irony was that when the hero groups died off, the world kept spinning. Why? Who the fuck cares? It just proved that we didn't need them anymore. It was funny because when the heroes were taken out, most of the costumed villains hung up their capes and retired with a profound sense of closure.

Of course, killing all of your enemies tends to do that very thing.

"Eight more minutes," Grace announced as she sat down at the terminal.

"Where was their main base?" Forecast asked.

Dirtnap nostalgically grinned down at her. "*The Argus* was this secret, floating fortress that was protected by a giant force bubble. It teleported to a different part of the world every 12 hours."

"It sounds awesome!" Forecast smiled. "Where is it now?"

The grizzled shooter's face fell. He didn't want to say it. Forecast was about to ask again –

"It's in tiny pieces at the bottom of the Pacific," I bluntly told her.

"Oh," Forecast said as her smile went away.

"You run a diagnostic on this place?" I asked, ignoring Dirtnap's scolding glare.

"First thing I did," Grace replied. "All systems are up and running."

The terminal's workstation hummed to life as I leaned over her right shoulder.

"While we're waiting, maybe you should tell us about this 'mystery threat' to the city," I whispered.

CHAPTER FIFTEEN

Grace sighed and looked up at me. Even though we were "partners" in this little nightmare, she still didn't trust me.

"A week ago, I got a tip from an old contact," Grace haltingly began. "He told me that today, sometime before dawn, Pillar City would be obliterated."

I blinked and then looked down at Teke, whose mouth fell open.

"And who'd you warn about this?!" Teke asked.

"I'd have warned everyone . . . if I had any idea of what the threat was," Grace insisted. "He promised to have more intel ready for me when I arrived."

"Clearly, that plan didn't work," I sighed. "Lemme guess . . . your snitch is dead and the intel's nowhere to be found?"

"Something like that," Grace said with regret in her eyes.

"What did he need you for?" I asked.

"He wanted me to psi-hack through a high-end firewall. Something only a handful of psi-hackers could crack," Grace continued.

"Did he give you anything to go on?" Dirtnap asked. "Anything we can use?"

"Ratiapp and I checked his condo but came up blank. Same for his e-mails. Then I remembered our old dead drop."

Grace reached into her blouse, under her bra, and pulled out a folded slip of white paper.

"That's where I found this."

I took it from her and opened it up. As I did, I noticed that the paper had a few drops of dried blood on it:

Grace,

If you're reading this, assume I'm dead. Don't worry about me. Worry about the city. All I know for sure's that the threat's gonna come from the water. Sometime before dawn on the 13th. I overheard all of that and a code: 414A987#V. Don't know what the code's for.

Please figure this out, Grace. Warn the world when you do. The threat's real and I'm out of time.

Good luck.

V.

I passed the note to Teke as Dirtnap and Forecast crowded behind him to read it. Grace locked eyes with me, silently pleading for me to believe her thin-assed story. Deep in thought, I set the wakizashi on top of the server and began to pace.

If not for Ratiapp, I would've kicked Grace Lexia out of my new lair and worried about my own fucking troubles. The thing is, I owed the man my life. Since I hated owing anyone, the least I could do for the late Mr. Ratiapp (and his next of kin) was to look into this so-called "threat."

"Who's this source?" I asked.

Grace allowed herself a sigh of relief.

"Back when I was a cop, he used to be one of my low-rent CI's. I hadn't heard from him since I left the force."

"What was he into?" I asked.

Grace hesitated, unsure of whether or not to give up his name—

"It's Vincent Mockre, isn't it?" Forecast asked, out of nowhere. "'V' for Vincent?"

I stopped in my tracks as Grace nodded.

Oh this changed things!

Mockre must've been investigating this threat for months, which explained his surveillance gear. Somewhere along the line, the O'Flernans noticed him poking around and suspected him of being a traitor. That's why they had my firm look into him. Then I blew his cover.

Maybe he was a federal snitch, working to bring down the O'Flernans, when he stumbled across a terror threat of some kind. Still, Seamus' guys tortured Mockre for days, used telepaths, and got nothing out of him. Why wouldn't he talk?! If millions of lives were at stake (including his own), the fucker should've told Seamus everything . . .

Or maybe he did.

Seamus was freaked-out at the *Versantio*, which suggested that someone told him something. Seamus had enough connections to verify the threat on his own . . . which was how he must've learned about The Black Wheel. He sent Ronns to *The Depravity* to keep him out of harm's way. If he believed someone was out to blow up his city, Seamus might even have called in the feds. He had enough juice to have three agents assigned to back him up—agents I killed.

So much for my *No children, no feds* rule.

Still, the feds didn't—or couldn't—act on the intel, which made no fucking sense. After 9/11, every agency under the sun should be scouring this city. Short on time, Seamus tried to hire me to kill these Black Wheel fuckers. Only his offer was too full of holes. Then everything went to shit. Before Pinpoint killed him,

Seamus was ranting about how we'd all end up dead if I didn't take the job.

None of that explained the psi-screen in Mockre's head, though. Anything that good wouldn't be in the head of a mere mobster or federal informant. Maybe that's why Seamus had him tortured, de-tongued, and murdered. Just like me, he wanted to see who'd come to save Mockre –

"Now what?" Dirtnap asked, dragging my mind back to the present.

I looked down at my Rolex. It was 3:54 a.m., which left us with three hours (tops). Everyone hopefully looked my way as I resumed my circular pacing.

"What did your guys come up with?" I sighed. "Mitch and Seth?"

"You mean before they ran?" Grace replied with disgust, "Mitch figured that the code was meant to disarm the weapon—possibly a WMD of some kind. He did manage to pull your cell phone call with Gratte, which led me to you. Seth's contacts checked the waterfronts but came up dry."

"You sure about that?" Dirtnap asked. "Mockre specifically mentioned 'water' in his note. As for your buddies, they sound about as reliable as my daddy's rubber."

Grace suppressed a grin as she focused on the screen.

"Fine. I'll scan the local waters," she offered.

Holomaps of Pillar City appeared over the server. Some were 3-D images. Others were live satellite imagery. We shut up and let her work.

A few minutes passed.

"I've got something," Grace said with a surprised frown. "There's a shielded fusion core under the water. It's about fourteen miles out. If its course doesn't change, it should arrive at the North Docks within the hour."

"Is it a sub?" Teke asked.

"Way too big," Grace shook her head.

"Show me," I leaned over her left shoulder.

A 3-D holographic display of Uptown's North Docks appeared out of thin air and then expanded in size. Just offshore, a flashing blue sphere appeared. The image shifted to reveal the 3-D representation of a gray-hulled vessel near the ocean floor. Its design vaguely reminded me of a giant metal tick. More than ten stories high, it had no visible means of propulsion.

Yet it moved.

"Looks like a sub to me," Dirtnap frowned.

"More like a mobile base," Grace replied, genuinely intrigued. "I'm counting ten active decks and external weaponry. Going after their data core . . ."

We crowded around Grace as she attempted to gain access. The psi-hacker sat motionless for over a minute before she leaned back into her chair with a frustrated sigh.

"I think this was the 'high-end firewall' Vince mentioned," Grace conceded.

"Not to mention your mystery threat, " Teke added. "Can you get in?"

"Their encryption tech's Russian . . . and very advanced. Even if I had the right passwords, I can't breach from the outside without tripping all kinds of alarms."

"How much time would you need?" Teke asked.

"From the outside? Without an interface?" Grace paused to do the math. "Maybe half an hour. But by then, they'll track us here."

"Wait," I swallowed, "This ship's Russian?"

"I'm not an expert on ship design," Grace looked up at me. "But the encryptions are definitely Russian."

Grace looked up and noticed the look of dread on my face.

"You know what it is?" Forecast asked.

"That's a floating weapons lab for the Povchenko Mob," I explained.

That's when everyone else got scared. The Povchenkos messed with every conceivable type of weapon—from advanced firearms to planet-killing munitions. One of their WMDs going off was scary enough. Should all of them blow up at once . . .

"About three years ago," I explained, "the Povchenkos hired Gratte to design a 'theoretical' construct: a model for a full-scale R&D facility. Gratte told me that it was to become a mobile lab, where they could build and test some of their experimental weaponry."

"What kind?" Grace asked. "Nuclear? Biological?"

"And then some," I quietly replied. "Gratte and his team worked up the specs and sent them to the Russians. He later heard that they had abandoned the project; some bullshit about it being 'too expensive to operate.'"

Dirtnap gently chewed on his lower lip, "We need eyes in there."

"Get me aboard," Grace offered, "and I could take the ship in under three minutes –"

"– if they don't blow your head off by then," Dirtnap muttered.

He was right. It was safe to assume that a small army of Russian mobsters (human and superhuman) protected the lab. Odds were that Spetrovich installed automated defenses as well.

Breaking into Fort Knox would be just a bit easier.

"Sync up this gear," I said. "I need encrypted comms."

"What are you gonna do?" Grace nervously asked.

"Break in and set up a remote interface," I offered.

Grace blinked, bothered that she hadn't thought of that option.

"If it's linked to this server, I could take the ship in under thirty seconds," Grace assured me.

"Okay then," I said with a brief smile. "Let's be pirates."

CHAPTER SIXTEEN

"Don't we have enough proof to give the feds a call?" Forecast asked, clearly worried about me. "Couldn't they take care of this?"

"By the time we convinced the right people, it might be too late," I replied.

"Besides, the Russkies would kill us for outing their little secret," Dirtnap added. "We wouldn't want that."

Heading for the nearest supply shelf, I stopped in front of its transparent barrier and cleared my throat. Grace took the hint and closed her eyes. The barrier slid open (as did barriers in front of other shelves as well). Beyond them were gadgets and weapons aplenty. Shelf lighting popped on inside. I grabbed an earpiece and clamped it around my right ear.

"We're synced," Grace said. "Encrypting comms now."

In front of me were ten small gray boxes labeled ENTRY SUITS. I grabbed one and opened it. One of the few things I liked about the ArgoKnights was that they were prepped for damned near any type of crisis. Entry suits were a classic example.

Packed full of nanites, the device turned into a one-size-fits-all armor with amazing durability and freedom of movement. Entry suits were designed as a sort of armored life support unit. It allowed the heroes to wade into toxic areas (even outer space) and fight evil, without cramping their style. Since some of the ArgoKnights needed their costumes in the field, the skin-tight entry suits could be worn under any type of clothing.

I opened the box. Inside was a metal, dome-shaped activation device with a white button on top. Small enough to fit in the palm of my left hand, this tech was one-of-a-kind. Since *Clean Sweep*, I've seen reverse-engineered variants of entry suits. On the street, they were called PBAs ("Push-Button Armor"). Most folks considered them to be decent tech. In reality, they were a nice try and nothing more.

When was the last time you broke into anything, Cly? Teke telepathically asked.

I turned to find the old man giving me his patented look of skepticism.

I've still got a few powers in my system, remember?

You're forgetting the metalform, which gave out mid-fight. That should scare you a bit, kid.

I've made do so far, Teke. My augments were supposed to break down after twenty years. It's been twenty-two.

You were also able to rip fifty powers—at a glance—for up to a week at a time! Your augments are slipping into pre-failure stage –

They've been that way for years, Teke.

You know what I mean, Cly! Five minutes after those augments fail, your organs shut down and you are dead! Get to that point and not even a dozen healers could save you.

Why do you think I sat on my ass and got fat for ten years?! The less I use my powers, the longer my augments last.

Have any of your power rips ever failed before tonight?

No. They haven't.

I'm not saying you're not good enough to do this, Teke relented. *Just ease off your augments or you'll drop dead in the middle of the fucking mission.*

Yessir.

We swapped tense grins as Dirtnap walked over.

"Even though you're a closet badass, you can't pull this off alone," Dirtnap said as he eyed the shelves' contents. "Take me with you."

I looked over at Dirtnap and sighed.

"If the security grid falls and a breaching team comes through that door, who has the biggest gun in the room? That would be you."

Dirtnap started to reply but chose not to. I unbuttoned my vest with the activation device still in my hand.

"And don't forget what Ronns said at that meeting," Teke added. "Whoever's seen working with Cly is marked for death."

"He's right," Forecast added. "Think of your fam."

Dirtnap's stubborn visage melted as he folded his arms and turned away.

"And, uh, I'm too fucking adorable to die," Teke joked.

Chuckling, I unbuttoned my shirt halfway.

"Anything else?" Grace asked.

"Record my actions."

"Like you did at *The Versantio*?"

"Yeah," I replied. "In case I have to explain my actions to the cops or the mobs."

"Community Service?" Forecast asked.

"Something like that," I nodded. "To save the city, I might have to sink that bath toy. If I do, I'll need proof that I did it for a good reason."

"I could rig some prober cams to follow you around," Grace offered.

"Do it," I said.

Then I slapped the activation device against my bare chest—button outward.

"It looks like a keyboard mouse," Dirtnap scoffed. "How do you know that crap's still gonna work?"

I gave him a shrug and pressed the button.

Dirtnap backed away as the activation device exploded around me. Nanomesh flew out like a harmless white mist. Then, after a second or two, it zipped under my clothes and turned solid. Three seconds later, I was covered head-to-toe in a form-fitting entry suit. I headed for a section of wall that was reflective enough to serve as a mirror. As I buttoned up my shirt and vest over the entry suit, I gave myself a quick once-over.

To the untrained eye, the armor looked to be nothing more than a thin, light-gray body suit. The ArgoKnight logo was emblazoned across my chest. There weren't any openings in the suit but I could breathe and see through the opaque material just fine. Potty breaks would have to wait, I guess. Like my old armor, the entry suit came with a built-in life support feature (with a three-hour duration).

"Batman's got nothing on you, Cly," Teke teased.

I gave him the finger and went after more supplies.

"What if you run into Spetrovich?" Dirtnap asked. "That weasel could end you with the press of a button, right?"

"These are 'dumb' nanites," Grace explained. "Unhackable. Most of this old gear is."

"Can't all nanodevices be hacked?" Forecast argued.

"Only if it's designed to receive signals," Grace patiently explained. "This armor's nanites can only do X number of things. Psi-hacking it would be like trying to psi-hack an old toaster or an electric shaver."

"Unless you built some kind of interface," I countered.

"Yeah," Grace conceded.

"Could a psi-hacker get in?" Teke asked. "Like, by touching the armor?"

Grace pursed her lips for a moment.

"Nah," she replied with the strangest smile.

A pair of silvery metal ovals floated out of another supply shelf. Each about the size of a football, I watched them assume stationary positions over my shoulders. ArgoKnight prober cams were useful little platforms with 1,001 features—like interface tech or the ability to record my every move. I had planned to strap one on my back but her idea was better.

"Now these prober cams can be hacked," Grace told Forecast. "But they're slaved to Cly and will respond to his verbal commands."

Then she turned my way.

"They'll start streaming when you get there. I'd appreciate it if you didn't mention us," Grace said.

I nodded. She knew that any footage I gave to the mobs would be gone over in minute detail. The last thing any of us wanted was for them to see the inside of this Way Station or ID my team.

My team.

Heh! Next, I'll be starting my own hero group.

I grabbed a utility sash and slipped it over my head. It ran diagonally from right-to-left. The moment I put it on, the sash tightened around my shirt and vest without blocking the shoulder holsters. I put my suit jacket back on as the sash self-locked. Empty sash pouches began to sprout from the gadget-carrying device.

I started filling them up.

"You know how to use that stuff?" Grace asked.

"When studying your enemy, know his tools," I replied as I grabbed a handful of red marble grenades.

"How are you breaching?" Dirtnap asked with his eyes on Grace.

"The same way I breached the basement," I grinned under my new mask.

I slipped a pair of red sensor goggles over my covered eyes. Thick and round, they reminded me of Steampunk goggles or something a welder might use. They flickered on and fed me passive read-outs of the Way Station and everyone in it.

"If you have to blow it up," Grace announced, "you need to get that thing more than 20 miles from shore."

"That's the minimum safe distance?" I asked.

"For the fusion core only? Yes," Grace estimated, her eyes on the terminal. "But if there's a large enough stockpile of high-megaton nukes in there . . ."

"Understood."

"I also wouldn't be surprised if the auto-destruct has to be manually set," Teke added.

"Yeah," I muttered. "Can't have this being any easier than it already is."

"Won't alarms go off the second you step onboard?" Dirtnap asked.

I didn't expect to have the element of surprise. Odds were that the ship had sentries, sensors, and/or booby traps all over the place. I should stumble into a firefight about a minute after I breached.

"I could just make stuff 'malfunction' as needed," Grace offered.

"Please do," I replied.

Dirtnap smiled as he held out his hand.

"Fancy duds or not, you're in for a messy death."

"You've really gotta work on your good luck speeches," I laughed as we shook hands.

During the brief contact, I resisted the urge to rip his phasing ability. He might need it.

"Just proves I'm sane," Dirtnap replied with a wry grin.

Forecast grabbed my wakizashi off the server and handed it to me with her left hand.

"Keep 'em safe, eh?" I grinned.

Still worried about me, Forecast cradled her MP5 with both hands. I eyed my blade and briefly wondered where I'd find a scabbard for it. Checking the shelves for anything else I might need, I noticed a stack of flight collars.

Each flight collar was designed to only respond to the verbal commands of its wearer. Like the entry suit, it couldn't be hacked without an interface. Too bad its internal AI wasn't smart enough to independently act. I'd have to give it verbal maneuvering commands, much like I would a trained dog.

"You're breaking into a Russian super base of some kind," Grace said. "Don't you need something better than a fancy knife?"

I easily stabbed the wakizashi's tip through the metallic floor and left it there.

"It won't jam like a gun," I explained as I pulled out a dull gray flight collar and clamped it around my neck. "It won't make much noise. Nor will it ever run out of ammo. Besides, if I need a gun, I'll just borrow one of the crew's weapons."

"He is breaking into a floating armory," Dirtnap added.

Grace chuckled as I retrieved my wakizashi. I suddenly remembered that my utility sash had a magnetic clamp on the back end. I carefully tapped the flat of the weapon against the back of the sash. The wakizashi stuck to it securely enough. If I needed to pull it, the sash would let me.

"How do I look?" I asked as I tugged on the lapels of my Armani.

"You could almost pass for one of the good guys," Grace teased.

"Don't insult me," I joked.

"What do we do while you're gone?" Forecast asked.

"Watch each other's backs—and mine," I replied. "By the way, give Teke a reading of his future. Say . . . the next twelve hours?"

Forecast nodded.

I never let Forecast give me future readings because they were worse than an ice cream headache times ten. The deeper into the future one looked, the more it hurt. Still, a sneak-peek of the future made plenty of sense right now. Forecast walked over to Teke and playfully rubbed her hands across his hair. Annoyed, Teke let her.

Then he flinched as the vision slammed into his mind, much like an artificial flashback. Teke took it all in . . . then he looked up at me with absolute dread.

"What is it?" Forecast asked, worried by the telepath's reaction to her vision.

"We need a better plan," Teke sighed.

CHAPTER SEVENTEEN

Teke closed his eyes and shot a copy of Forecast's vision into our minds. It was never good when her visions came with a birds-eye view. It usually meant that the person who had said vision (namely Teke) was already dead. The view was of Pillar City in the pre-dawn hours. Traffic flowed and planes soared overhead.

Curious as to how Teke died, I looked over at him.

"You skipped ahead about an hour," I realized. "Why?"

"Because it's not as relevant as what comes next," came Teke's cryptic reply. "Now shut up and watch."

I frowned as he turned to Grace.

"Make a holoimage of this and record it."

Given the right tech, psi-hackers could convert their memories or even daydreams into digital files. Maybe Teke wanted "proof" of whatever this threat was. Still, no one would believe it unless they knew Forecast and how her powers worked.

"Why?" Grace frowned. "No one's gonna believe – "

"Just do it," Teke irritably snapped.

A paused holoimage (exactly like the one in our heads) appeared over the server. Teke sized it up for a moment, gave it a nod of satisfaction, and resumed the psi-show. The holoimage streamed along as he did.

So far, things looked calm. It was just like any other Saturday morning –

A fiery-gray mushroom cloud erupted from the ocean. It expanded in all directions, while soaring toward the sky. There was no massive blast wave, which should've flattened everything around it. It engulfed Pillar City but didn't spread any further. Even *The Depravity* was left untouched.

"So much for a false alarm," I sighed.

"That's not a standard nuke blast," Dirtnap said.

Teke paused the vision in our heads, while Grace paused it on the server.

"I've seen one of these before," he grimly explained. "It's a HN blast."

"Hydronemesis?" I groaned.

Teke nodded.

"A what?" Forecast asked.

"It's a reusable warhead," Teke explained, "capable of absorbing all of the moisture within a set area. The Taiwanese designed them as a defense against a Chinese invasion."

"So . . . it evaporates all the water for miles around?" Dirtnap asked.

Teke nodded. "Anything liquid gets turned into steam—whether it's organic or not."

The implications were scary, seeing as Pillar City wasn't a natural island. It was originally built atop a massive mechanical platform with thirty-four hydroelectric thrusters underneath. Nicknamed "The Pillars," they held the entire island at the waterline with a steady, invisible field of anti-gravity. These massive devices were built by the same geniuses who designed Downtown's synthetic sky.

Once called the "Eighth Wonder of the World," these unique thrusters ran solely on hydroelectric power. Somehow, they drew in water, generated a base amount of energy, and then amplified it many times over. I don't understand the physics but The Pillars were designed to adjust for the city's gradual increases in both size and weight. The hydroelectric systems generated so much extra energy that they also fueled Pillar City's entire power grid.

Teke gave us rest of the vision with Grace recording in the background.

Without a shitload of ocean to power those circular thrusters, Pillar City dropped straight down. Shaped like a giant slice of layer cake, the dying metropolis hit the dry earth below, where it was crushed under its own weight. Uptown crumbled into Downtown. Explosions—big and small—dotted the island city. The HN's blast field kept the ocean at bay for several seconds. Then the mushroom cloud abruptly lost its fury and began to dissipate.

That's when the water rushed in.

It was a safe assumption that there weren't any survivors. Millions of people were instantly evaporated. Any supers lucky enough to survive the initial blast probably got crushed by the city and/or drowned by the waves. Teke fast-forwarded the vision over the remaining twelve hours, showing first-responders and media swarming over the scene. Nothing but debris resurfaced. Some of it belonged to the Russian ship.

Then the vision went black.

"Holy shit!" Forecast gasped. "Where'd that come from?!"

"Language!" I scolded her. Then I turned to Grace. "Was that an auto-destruct?"

Horrified at watching her hometown die, Grace could only shrug as she stopped the recording.

"At least nothing else blew up," I muttered, thinking of the ship's fusion core, defensive weapons, and arms cache.

"This time, we go in as a team and kill these fuckers!" Dirtnap scowled.

I paused to weigh the factors involved.

Judging from the image, the blast was just over an hour from now. I didn't have time to argue this with them. Forecast was untested. Dirtnap and Grace weren't good enough to survive this kind of raid. While more than capable, Teke was done with black ops.

"Grace, run a diagnostic on the teleportation grid," I told her. "Then pull everything you can on Hydronemesis warheads—especially disarming them."

"Will do," she replied. "I'll slip a copy into your prober cams, just in case."

"Won't they have teleportation jammers?" Forecast frowned.

"Probably," I replied. "That's why I'll have to go in first and give Grace her interface link. Then she can kill their jammers, allowing you all to teleport in and back me up."

"Sounds crazy enough to work," Grace agreed, still shaken by the looming genocide.

"Then gear up. We head out in ten," I ordered as I patted Dirtnap's left shoulder and ripped his phasing ability.

He followed my gaze as I nodded toward the downward stairwell. "Secure the lower levels, huh?"

"About time you started acting sensible," Dirtnap smiled as he drew Junior and headed downstairs.

Forecast all but grinned at the thought of getting into the shit for the first time. I walked over and rubbed my right hand through her hair.

"Calm down, kid," I said as I ripped her power.

"What do you need me to do?" Forecast eagerly asked.

"Grab all the shit you can carry."

"On it," she rushed to comply.

Oh, you fucking bastard! Teke resignedly psi-muttered as he reached out and bumped fists with me.

You can tag along, if you want.

No thanks. I've used up all nine of my fucking lives, kid. Just get out of there in one piece, eh?

Our fists still touching, I ripped his telekinesis but left his other powers alone.

Teke blinked with surprise.

Take the rest, Cly! You might need 'em –

Seeing as you die before the bomb goes off, so might you. What are you hiding from me?

We get ambushed the moment you leave.

That sucks, because I have to leave real soon. What happens next?

Overwhelming numbers, a messy fight, and then I'm dead. Didn't even see it coming.

Follow my lead, then. First, I have to rip Grace –

I'd leave her shit alone, Cly. Teke nervously warned me. *A power that unstable might bring you down.*

No choice, old man. If this site's getting raided, Grace can't hack the ship by remote. If I bring her along, she's dead in the initial crossfire. Unless you've got any better ideas?

No, Teke psi-grumbled.

Grace looked up as I casually strolled over.

"Mind if I bum a Glock off you? I might need an extra gun after all."

Grace was fooled for a half-second. She started to reach for the Glock on her right hip. Then she noticed my two handguns and outstretched right hand. Her eyes widened.

"Don't!" Grace yelled as she whipped out her shoulder-holstered Glocks and scrambled away from me.

She aimed them at my masked face with trembling hands, as if I was Death in a suit. Grace knew that she couldn't stop me from ripping her powers. That her bullets wouldn't breach my entry suit. Yet, she was terrified about what would happen if I ripped her.

"What?" Forecast asked with her weapon half-raised.

"That ship has a top-notch firewall, Cly!" Grace argued. "Even with my power, you're not skilled enough to hack it!"

Gal's got a point.

I ignored Teke as I slowly sat down in Grace's chair and folded my arms.

"What if the interface signal is (somehow) jammed?" I pointedly asked. "Then you can't help me. The bomb goes off. We all die."

Grace bit down on her trembling lower lip.

"If you rip me, Cly, that might happen anyway."

The psi-hacker slowly holstered her guns.

"If they use interface jammers, I'll find a way past them," she stubbornly promised. "I can do it."

Think she could pull it off?

No.

"Fine," I muttered. "We'll do it your way."

I hopped out of the chair and walked over to Forecast. She expectantly looked up at me.

"You gonna rip me too?" she asked with a nervous smile.

"Wouldn't dream of it," I lied as I tapped her forehead.

I gave Forecast a full vision of the next 12 hours of her life. The precog staggered back under the pain of her first vision. In spite of the discomfort, she smiled at seeing her own future for the first time . . . and then shuddered. Whatever she saw scared the shit out of –

"Grenade!" Forecast yelled as she deftly sprayed the far corner of the room.

Wakizashi at the ready, I spun toward the direction of her gunfire and noticed the blood splatter. Most of her thirty rounds hit an invisible someone. I pulled my left-holstered Walther and handed it to her. She dropped the MP5, snatched the gun from my hand, and racked the slide.

A few seconds later, the corpse of Doug Jausse flickered into view. Dressed in gray-and-black fatigues, sparks emerged from his chest as he slumped to the floor. Some of Forecast's shots hit his face, revealing the metal underneath. The cyborg stared up at us in lifeless shock. A can-shaped stun grenade rolled out of his left hand, with the pin still attached. Had I left, he could've dropped everyone else with the element of surprise and a well-placed throw.

Even more troubling was that the late Mr. Jausse used to work for me. The former Army Ranger had himself outfitted with cyberimplants (which made him invisible to human senses, tech, and even psychics). With ocular implants in both eyes, he was one of my best surveillance specialists. Whatever he saw and heard could be recorded or streamed like a live camera feed.

"Is he transmitting?"

Grace narrowed her eyes.

"Yep. Jamming his systems now."

Dirtnap ran up the stairs with Junior drawn.

"What's goin' on?!"

He paused and gawked at Jausse's corpse.

"What's he doin' here?!"

"Bleeding on my floor," came my distracted reply. "Grace, pull a sensor sweep of the area."

The psi-hacker stared off for a few seconds.

"Sensors are down . . . along with the Way Station's defense grid."

"I thought you ran a diagnostic!" Dirtnap shouted.

"I did!" Grace snapped. "Somehow, both systems got sabotaged."

"I think your friends are here," I told Teke. "How many?"

"I stopped counting at 57 hostiles," he replied with a worried smile. "Most of them are supers and I think they all used to kill for you, Cly."

"This what you saw in your vision?" Grace asked.

"Not really. I was shot in the head at this point," Teke meekly replied.

"What about Ray?" Forecast asked. "Is he all right?"

She didn't get it—yet.

Only Ray could've mobilized so many of my guys against me so goddamned fast. I'd say that Jausse slipped in here when Ray was "fixing" the server (and sabotaging the defense grid and sensors). With eyes and ears in the room, the speedster could orchestrate an ambush with ease.

Lucky for us, Ray decided to wait for me to leave. When Teke had Grace make a holoimage of the blast, he also bought us some time. Ray would believe the threat and react accordingly. I looked over at the lair's only entrance. Teke had wrecked the door controls when he got us in here. Now that it was closed again, it should keep them out for a while (I hope).

My burner phone rang. I flipped it open, put it on SPEAKER, and waved the others away from the entrance.

"Nice try," I said with an even tone. "Jausse almost got it done."

"So I saw," Ray replied with admiration. "Your mix of luck, friends, and brains is impressive, Cly."

Forecast's face fell as she realized Ray's betrayal.

"So what now?"

"Give up," Ray replied. "Teke and Dirtnap might walk away from this—but not the ladies."

I looked over at Grace.

"You're after the price on her head?"

"That's part of it," he admitted. "Then there's Grace's value to The Black Wheel. Clearly, they're behind the bounty. I turn her in and maybe I'll figure out who they are. Since they're trying to blow up my city, they have to die."

"Your plan sounds thin," I frowned.

"Don't worry, Cly. I'll make it work."

"What about Forecast?"

"A true-blue precog's a priceless tactical asset," Ray said. "You were smart to keep her powers under wraps."

"You're gonna sell her?!" Dirtnap scowled.

"God no!" Ray chuckled. "With Forecast at my side, who could stop me?"

Forecast's teary eyes shifted toward her MP5, then over to Jausse—her first kill. That realization was sinking in hard and fast.

"You want to take over my operations?" I asked with a hateful edge. "Or just run the city?"

"Yes on both counts," Ray replied. "As far as schemes go, this one's pretty good. Think about it. I cash in on Grace. I've got a sizeable group of your best killers to work for me. Forecast shows me the future when I need to see it. I'll deliver you to the O'Flernans and sell some samples of your DNA on the black market. I'd make at least $60 million for a few hours' work. Best of all, I establish myself as this town's top fixer."

"What about the bomb?" I asked.

"We've got an hour to stop the warhead," replied the arrogant fuck. "That gives me plenty of time to send two teams to disarm it. Naturally, I'll take full credit for saving the day."

"What about Teke and Dirtnap?" Grace asked.

"I was going to kill them," Ray confessed. "Of course, Cly could save their lives."

I looked over at Teke, who angrily shook his head. Given the chance, the old man would've simply erased Ray's mind right then and there. Knowing this, the speedster had either just activated a psi-shield or gotten out of the telepath's six-mile range.

"What do you want?"

"Spetrovich wrecked your main server, Cly. Knowing you, there's a backup somewhere. I want its location and access code."

Clever boy.

I did have a backup server. It was hidden within the Internet itself, easily accessible by computer or cell phone. Scattered across tens of millions of websites, it copied files from my armor's server every three hours. With my armor destroyed, it would've slipped into passive mode. The only way to unify the server files and access them was with my password (known as a "frag code"). If Ray got it, he could replace me without missing a beat.

I started to turn him down –

"Fuck you!" Forecast screamed into the phone.

Shocked as hell, I could only watch as she snatched it from my hand and hung up. She angrily flung it aside and broke down crying. I wrapped my right arm around the sobbing child and held her close. I tried to think of something comforting to say—

"Think they'll stop the bomb in time?" Grace urgently asked as she picked up the Uzi.

I started to shake my head when the lair's entry door was suddenly knocked inward.

In stepped Pugil.

Short for "pugilist," the natural-born super loved to brawl. At 6'4", the tanned brute was the strongest contractor I had ever recruited. I once saw him level a thirty-story building in under a minute. Then there was the time he chewed up a diamond—just to prove he could.

Pugil wasn't ex-military or a former black ops specialist. No, he was a force of nature, with the physique of a body builder and the mindset of a bully. Still, whenever I needed someone extracted from a hairy location (friend or foe), I'd send Pugil along (as a distraction). He'd make an unholy mess, kill a lot of people, and get the job done.

Tonight, Pugil was bare-chested, with black muscle pants and matching boots. A coarse, two-foot braid of red hair ran down his massive back. His stern, bearded face tightened as he noticed Jausse's corpse. He started to say something, when three of my former contractors rushed into the mix with weapons drawn.

Fortunately, Dirtnap was the fastest gun in the room. Junior turned all three of Ray's guys into gooey chunks, while leaving three small craters in the wall behind them. With a snarl, Dirtnap then aimed at Pugil and gave him five rounds to the chest.

Shell casings hit the floor as we all winced from the roar of Dirtnap's hand cannon. Not only was Pugil still alive, he hadn't budged an inch. He simply looked down at his unblemished chest and then sneered at us.

"I've got this," the super casually declared as he signaled the rest of his backup team to stay in the tunnel.

Without even a hint of guilt, he walked over to kick our asses. I stepped in front of Dirtnap and pulled an ice disc from my utility sash. When thrown, the quarter-sized disc would explode on impact with any tangible surface. Then it would release a fast-freezing cryogas that would harden into a synthetic white ice. Unless it was shattered or melted, the ice could last indefinitely. Designed to put out fires or block up holes, most gadget-carrying ArgoKnights swore by them.

Pugil recognized the weapon and shook his head.

"That won't stop me," he bragged.

"Good-bye, Pugil," I sighed as I flicked the ice disc at his chest.

Used to things bouncing off his nigh-invulnerable body, Pugil didn't bother to avoid it. The poor guy might've tried if he knew that I had phased the ice disc when I threw it. Or that it would stay phased when it left my hand—for a split-second, anyway. It was phased just long enough to pass through his chest, turn solid again, bounce off his insides, and then explode. Pugil's face twisted with disbelieving agony . . . and then he was a statue, of sorts.

Jagged icicles erupted from his mouth, eyes, nose, ears, and even his asshole.

"That was cold, Cly!" Dirtnap frowned, unaware of his own pun.

Sounds of gunfire, screams, and energy attacks suddenly raged above us. Confused, I looked over at Teke, who seemed a bit "distracted." The mischievous telepath gave me a knowing grin.

"What's going on up there?" Dirtnap asked, gun tightly clenched in his right hand.

"Half of Ray's guys—the ones with weak minds— suddenly 'decided' to kill the other half," came the telepath's blunt reply. "Get us out of here, please?!"

"On it," I said as I pulled out another ice disc and flung it into the entrance.

The cryogas expanded and created a temporary ice barrier. That's when I felt an initial twinge of nausea. I had ripped more powers than my system could handle. The more I used them, the worse it would get.

Fuck!

"Grace, kill the overhead lights."

She turned them off with a whim. The only remaining lights came from the equipment shelves, which gave me plenty of shadows to choose from.

"Let's gear up," Dirtnap muttered as he holstered Junior.

"No time," I replied.

"Did you rip everybody else?" Grace griped.

"It made sense at the time," I shrugged.

With that, I opened a big-assed shadow portal. Then I telekinetically grabbed everything in the fucking room—whether it was bolted down or not—and sent it through to the other side. Grace and the others watched bits of ArgoKnight tech float harmlessly past them. I kept the prober cams around and left the bodies.

"Where's this stuff going?" Grace asked, as she snatched a floating pair of entry suit boxes out of the air.

"Someplace safe," I replied as the strain worsened.

A minute later, the room was cleared. Sweaty and tired, I then telekinetically picked Teke off his feet.

Cly! You're in pain. Ease off on the powers!

You know I can't. Tell Samir I said "hello" and then trade this vintage junk for his protection.

You won't last five minutes!

Then I'd better hurry. Keep her safe.

You can count on me, Heath.

I flinched at the mention of my real first name, one I had almost forgotten. Teke sadly waved as I sent him into the portal.

Dirtnap tumbled right after him, his arms and legs wildly thrashing.

"Cly!" Dirtnap yelled. "Are you crazy?! You can't do this alone!"

Then he was gone.

Forecast put my gun back into its holster. Then she gave me a parting hug. I affectionately rested my masked chin on top of her head.

"Did the bomb go off in your vision?" I asked her.

"Once the stun grenade went off, everything stayed black for the duration."

Ah. They kept her sedated.

"If you don't hear from me in two days, I'm dead or worse," I warned her. "Assume you're being hunted.

Remember your training. And no matter what happens kid . . . fight dirty. Promise?"

Forecast nodded with fresh tears in her eyes. She let me go and walked into the portal without looking back. It was just me and Grace. I narrowed the portal and changed its destination to that of the Russian ship –

"Kill the portal," Grace said.

"We need to leave right now."

"This'll just take a minute," she replied.

Curious, I shut down the portal. The pain in my skull eased off . . . a bit. Grace looked up from the entry suit boxes and held them out.

"Take them."

"Aren't you using one?" I frowned as I took them from her.

"I'm claustrophobic," Grace admitted. "Entry suits freak me out."

"Ah," I sighed. "So what do I do with these?"

"Just stand there," she smiled.

Both entry suit units suddenly exploded from within their boxes and wrapped around me in a double-sized white mist. Instead of instantly bonding to me (or my armor), the mist simply flowed around me.

"I'm already wearing an entry suit, Grace."

"Yeah," she nodded. "One made in 1981. I'm giving you an on-the-fly upgrade."

Really?

"How new is the tech?" I asked.

"This is The Outfitter's last version," Grace said, with a hint of reverence. "He had just finished field-testing it when he died."

The nanomist froze in mid-air, then flowed into my entry suit. I waited for something "cool" to happen . . . but nothing did.

"Now what?" I frowned under my mask.

"It's initializing," Grace said as she patted my chest. "You'll know when it's done."

"Fair enough," I shrugged as I opened a shadow tunnel.

The effort drove an even worse spike of pain through my head.

"You all right?" Grace asked, as I flinched.

"You comin' or not?" I grumbled.

Grace picked up her Uzi from floor and stepped close to me, this time without any reluctance. I wrapped my right arm around her waist. My left gripped the wakizashi. I walked Grace toward the portal while the prober cams followed us in. I figured this to be a one-way trip. I might live just long enough to get her on the ship and find the warhead.

After that, she'd be on her own.

The shadows swallowed us whole.

CHAPTER EIGHTEEN

Grace and I tumbled out of the shadow tunnel without incident. The prober cams formed up behind us as we found ourselves surrounded by bodies.

"This just keeps getting weirder," Grace frowned as she got up, Uzi gripped in both hands.

As I stood up and found myself covered in blood, I had to agree.

A one-sided massacre took place in this metallic, gray-walled corridor. The bullet-riddled bodies lay among thousands of spent shell casings. Remnants of explosions blackened the walls and ceiling (grenades, most likely). My goggles counted forty-one victims. Most of them had their limbs blown off. Only some of the overhead lighting survived the mayhem.

The silence was stifling.

"Povchenko mobsters?" Grace asked as she looked over the corpses.

"Yeah," I replied, surprised that they had a dress code.

The poor stiffs either wore red medical scrubs or gray-and-white paramilitary fatigues. Some were armed. Others weren't. With a gaze, I saw that five of the dead were supers (not that it saved them).

The sensor goggles gave me fresh updates. The read-out declared this crime scene to be 2.71 hours old. It also detected residual traces of inhibitor mist in the air. Worried, I gave Grace a quick once-over. While she had some of it on her clothes, only trace amounts were in her system—not enough to cut her powers off.

I scanned the walls and detected a honeycomb of concealed autoguns on either side. That's a damned naughty way to kill intruders. We'd have to assume that every deck was just as fucked up.

"What triggered the ship's security grid?" I asked.

"No idea," the ex-cop replied. "I'll tap the sensor logs once I'm through their firewall."

"Until then, stay close and don't touch anything," I warned her. "There are traces of inhibitor mist in here."

"Good to know," Grace replied as she lowered her weapon and closed her eyes. "Accessing the ship's server core."

We stood side-by-side, surrounded by slippery carnage and within easy walking distance of a WMD. There were definitely better ways to spend a Saturday morning.

"Trickier than I thought," she muttered after a few minutes of thoughtful psi-hacking.

"Try Mockre's mystery code," I suggested. "Maybe it's for the ship instead of the weapon."

Grace opened her eyes and looked my way.

"If it's not," she said, "you'd better be faster than these guns."

I clamped the wakizashi to the utility sash and then hooked her left arm in my right. If need be, I could phase us both in the blink of an eye. Still, the cozy gesture made her uneasy.

"Do your thing."

Grace nodded as she closed her eyes again. Seconds later, she smiled.

"I'm in. *The Red Gate's* under my thumb."

"That's the name of this shitcan?" I asked.

"Yeah," Grace said.

"Okay," I backed away. "The sensor logs can wait. Find Ray's people. I don't want them getting in our way."

"Are you going to kill them?"

"Depending on who Ray sent, I'm more worried about them killing us."

Her eyes still closed, Grace frowned.

"Aside from dead crew members, I've got nothing yet," she replied.

"What about reinforcements?" I asked. "This happened almost three hours ago. Povchenko has to know about this incident by now."

"Okay," Grace shrugged and narrowed her eyes. "Looking for any hint of a backup team . . . and nothing."

"We've gotta be missing something."

"I'll pull up the security footage."

The prober cams both hummed as multiple holoimages formed around us.

"Also, I'm tapping into the navigation controls," Grace mentioned as I looked for any sign of the HN warhead. "Should I take us out to sea?"

I bit down a grunt of pain. I felt my nose start to bleed.

"We'll be too busy to steer this thing around other ships. Bring it to a full-stop and kill the fusion core."

"Aye-aye, Captain Cly," she nervously joked. "Coming to a full-stop . . . now. Switching to auxiliary power. You want schematics?"

I nodded, impressed by Grace's usefulness.

As they came up, Grace moved in next to me and opened her eyes. We paused to study the ship. *The Red Gate* had ten decks and a crew compliment of 348. Deck One was the Bridge. Deck Two was Security. We were on Deck Three, which was the Medical Level. Decks Four and Five were the crew quarters.

Deck Six was Engineering. Deck Seven was the Machine Shop. Decks Eight and Nine were cargo holds. Deck Ten was the Brig. A network of six elevators ran along the ship's interior and accessed all levels. At first glance, *The Red Gate* wasn't designed for R&D. It was more like an amped-up weapons freighter.

"Whoa!" Grace exclaimed as the images for the cargo decks came up.

Someone had stripped *The Red Gate* clean. Both decks were lined with empty shelves.

"What was down there?" I asked.

"I'll look for a weapons inventory," Grace replied. "But why leave the warhead behind? To cover the theft?"

"Seems like overkill," I replied as I looked through images of Deck Nine's empty shelves. Designed to hold larger weapons and/or ordinance, the warhead to had to be –

"Found it!" Grace pointed at an ovular holoimage.

On Deck Nine (hidden behind some shelves) was one beige plastic crate with Cyrillic numbers with no other markings.

"According to the shipping manifest, the crate contains one newly-stolen Hydronemesis warhead," Grace smiled, relieved to have found the damned thing.

"Is it armed?"

Her smiled died.

"Pulling up sensors," Grace replied.

After a few seconds, she looked my way and nodded.

"Kill all power on that deck," I ordered.

"Why?"

"Disarming the warhead might set off the security grid," I replied as I kicked a dead guy's arm away from me. "We wouldn't want that now would we?"

"Good point," she admitted.

As Grace worked on Deck Nine, I was bothered by the fact that we were here first. Between a dead crew, stolen product, and a ticking warhead, Povchenko should've ordered a breach by now. I would've. He had supers. He had Spetrovich. They should've breached . . . so why didn't they?

"What the hell?!" Grace blinked.

"What?" I turned toward her.

"The system just locked me out –"

Inhibitor mist suddenly sprayed out of the ceiling above us. While the entry suit protected me, Grace wasn't so lucky. Blinded and coughing, she didn't see the hidden autoguns, which slid out of the walls (again) and opened fire. The assorted holoimages dissipated as both prober cams got shot to shit. Being only five feet away, I managed to crash-tackle Grace. As I phased us both, a howling volume of weapons' fire harmlessly whizzed through our bodies.

Tackling Grace sent us through the floor. Given enough momentum, gravity still affected phased matter. As we passed through ceilings and floors, inhibitor mist sprayed through us. We fell through each deck so fast that the autoguns couldn't track and fire. There was one small problem with phasing, though. Unless I countered our descent, we'd pass through the ship's underbelly and fall out into the ocean.

Luckily, I could fly.

I tapped the flight collar as we reached Deck Nine.

"Hover!" I yelled.

The flight collar vibrated against my throat and generated a field around me. Drenched in inhibitor mist, Grace coughed in my arms. We were 9.3 feet from the floor, according to the sensor goggles.

"Soft landing," I commanded.

The flight collar gently lowered us to the deck. The HN warhead was only a few yards away.

"You all right?" I groaned as I let her go.

Tangible again, Grace gave me a scowl as she continued coughing. I must've knocked the wind out of her. With the inhibitor mist in her lungs, she'd be powerless for the next six-to-twelve hours. Knowing this, Grace simply sat on the floor and emphatically pointed at the bomb.

Guess it was up to me now.

I reached into my utility sash and pulled out a mini-flare. Snapping the cigarette-shaped gadget in half, I tossed it against a corner wall. It erupted into a sustained, fiery-red brilliance that gave me plenty of large, useful shadows. I touched the crate and phased it. SpineSnapper's strength let me lob it aside with ease.

Inside was the Hydronemesis bomb. A bit smaller than the typical bathtub, the black, ovular WMD had a polished black metal surface. The warhead was also covered with Chinese lettering (serial numbers and warnings, mainly) and the Taiwanese flag. The digital display revealed 1:12:09 (and counting) on its digital countdown clock.

I telekinetically picked up the warhead.

The instant I moved the bomb, the sensor goggles registered a lethal shock along its surface. Unaffected, I continued to move it with my mind. The timer then beeped and began to countdown at an accelerated rate. Instead of 72 minutes (until detonation), I now had 72 seconds. I opened a shadow tunnel into the Marianas Trench and sent the warhead toward it.

Hopefully, no one was putzing around at the bottom of the ocean right now.

The warhead went in easily enough. As I watched it fall through the tunnel, a massive wave of agony hit me. It was so bad I dropped to my knees. The sensor goggles warned me of an imminent augmentation failure (no shit). Even with SpineSnapper's toughness, I was about to puke inside of this fucking costume. I cut off the phasing power and focused on keeping the tunnel open. If I blacked out, the HN warhead might pop out of any large shadow between here and there.

The warhead (finally) reached the other end. I closed the shadow tunnel and cut off the shadowporting power with a sigh of relief. Somehow, I stumbled to my feet.

"Okay," I gasped. "Day's saved. Let's get the fuck out of –"

My legs turned to yogurt and down I fell. Grace scrambled over to me with wide-eyed concern.

"Cly?!"

"Get out of here," I croaked as I watched my stolen powers fade away in random order.

I'll be damned! Never thought I'd die saving the world again –

CHAPTER NINETEEN

It's not easy playing possum.

The ability to regain consciousness—without a twitch or even a flickering of the eyes—is something of an exotic skill. Luckily, I hadn't lost my touch. Limp as a corpse, I took in my surroundings with my other senses. Someone was carrying my bulk over his right shoulder, as if I weighed next to nothing. Two more guys walked behind him with a relaxed stride.

Then there were the corpses.

Assuming we were still on *The Red Gate*, this ship was wall-to-wall with dead bodies, which would explain the stench. What bothered me was that I could actually smell the individual scents of the . . . sixty-four dead people in this corridor. My nose shouldn't be that acute.

What bothered me more was that I was ravenous. Granted, I hadn't eaten in almost twelve hours but this was different. It was like I hadn't eaten in fucking days. Even the horrid stench couldn't kill my appetite. With some difficulty, I took my mind off food and focused on the crisis at hand.

For some silly reason, they took off my entry suit but left me with my gadgets and weapons. Perhaps, they were staging my "corpse," trying to fool the Russians into thinking I was behind the weapons' theft. Eventually, they'd find their boat. It made sense to frame me for the raid.

Then there was the question of my guys—no, Ray's guys. Depending on how long I was down, they could've breached by now. He mentioned a pair of teams. Odds were that they'd enter from different points in the ship. Since Jausse was eavesdropping on us, he might've managed to record Mockre's note—and the master code.

However they breached, they'd find a shitload of dead Russian mobsters. The teams would bring (at least) one psi-hacker, who'd use the master code. Once in the ship's systems, he/she/they would tap into the sensors and look for the bomb. Within six or seven minutes, they'd get doused in inhibitor mist and shot to shit.

A clever trap.

Of course, they might've outwitted the ship's defenses. In fact, my ex-contractors could be lugging me around right now. Well, whoever my captives were, I could try to kill them and make a run for it. Too bad my odds of doing so (without getting shot) weren't that great. Frankly, it made more sense to play dead—for now. The trio stopped. I was casually dumped among a bunch of blood-soaked corpses. The guy who carried me casually drew a sidearm and racked the slide.

"Head or chest?" He asked one of his buddies.

"Head shot," chuckled the one on the left. "Make it sloppy."

Ah. They needed to make it look like I died mid-theft. So much for playing dead . . .

Just as I was about to feed him his gun, my fucking stomach growled loudly enough for all of them to hear. Fuck this! My eyes snapped open. I looked up and instantly knew that these guys were Black Wheel. Their thick white dusters and black ceramic body armor didn't settle it. Nor was it the fancy op tech they had on their persons.

No, their masks were a dead giveaway.

Each guy donned a metal combat mask. Similar to what hockey goalies wore, they were painted white with a red two-digit number on the right side. On the left was a five-spoked black wheel—the emblem of their outfit. I didn't know whether these guys were for-real or playing some kind of elaborate con. I just knew that it was time for them to die.

"What the hell?!" yelped #06, as his brown eyes widened behind his mask.

Bigger than the other two, #06 tried to shoot me with his sidearm—a suppressor-capped machine pistol. I tripped him up with my legs as he fired. His gun's wild, three-round burst harmlessly stitched the ceiling. As #06 fell, I drew the wakizashi with my right hand. By the time he fell on my blade, I had already aimed it for his heart.

It sank through his armor easily enough. Better still, he had practically dropped the machine pistol into my free hand. Side-by-side, #02 and #05 raised their fancy assault rifles. Even though I used their dying buddy as a human shield, they could've gotten me— until I fed them the rest of the mag.

Guess they were just too slow.

Alone at last, I shoved #06's heavy corpse off me with full gusto . . . and sent it flying? The body slammed into a wall (some thirty feet away) and slid to the floor with a broken neck. I had super strength, which made no sense. SpineSnapper's powers—along with the others—had failed before I blacked out. I looked down at my Rolex and saw that it was 8:51 a.m. Even if that augmentation failure didn't happen, all of my power rips should've expired by now.

I looked down and realized that my burger gut was gone. My torso looked . . . muscular, like a Greco-Roman wrestler. Bothered by the looseness of my clothes, I found myself sitting on a pile of familiar bodies—namely, my ex-contractors. Folks I would've picked for a job like this.

I stood up and glared down at them. None of these dead fucks deserved an ounce of regret. They knew the risks when they boarded this floating death trap. If the ship's defenses hadn't put them down, they might've killed Grace and me.

Or, they might've saved a city of millions on their own.

I should run. Assuming we were close to shore, I might even make it. The thing was I had me a genuine, honest-to-God chance to hurt The Black Wheel. To make that happen, I needed to know who they were and what they wanted. Here and now, someone on this ship had the answers I needed. Whoever it was deserved my full and violent attention.

I looked down at my hands to see if my core powers were truly gone. After such a massive augmentation failure, I should either be dead or reduced to a powerless human. To my surprise, the power gaze was still active. My other augmentations were gone, along with every power I had taken—except for the shadowportation. Somehow, it had permanently bonded to me. Stranger still, it evolved seven other abilities, much like branches growing out of a tree trunk.

What I saw frightened me (so much so that I tapped my goggles).

"Self-scan," I muttered with morbid disbelief.

The readouts popped up. I double-checked them before I shifted the wakizashi to my left hand and wiped it clean along my right sleeve. Then I carefully nicked the back of my right hand. My blood came out black. Under the harsh overhead lighting, it painfully sizzled like grease on a hot pan. The blood on my blade burned off just as fast. Then, after a few seconds, the wound closed before my fucking eyes!

"Replay the sensor logs of my mutation," I ordered with a quaking voice.

The goggle's sensor logs started at the point of my death, where Grace desperately tried to wake me up. She used the goggles to scan me. Then she tried—and failed—to get me out of my entry suit.

Frustrated, Grace Lexia dropped the goggles and did the damnedest thing. She just sat there and cried over me, something I'd never expect her to do. Grace should've gone for the Deck Nine escape pods and headed for shore. I had the goggles fast-forward to the part where a tranquilizer dart sank into the back of her neck.

Two Black Wheel grunts (#04 and #10) stepped past my waning mini-flare and carried her off, while leaving me to rot in the near-darkness. About a minute later, my entry suit began what the goggles described as an EMERGENCY VIRAL PURGE. The outfit basically broke down into the consistency of sand. Its nanites then flowed up my chest and into my mouth.

What. The. Fuck?!

80's-era entry suits weren't this advanced! Then I remembered Grace's software upgrades. While the nanites flooded my insides, my organs were rapidly mutating. Per the goggles, this mutation was caused by unknown microbes found in my lungs and bloodstream. If I had to guess, I'd say I "caught something" during one of my shadowportations.

As my augments were failing at the time, my immune system couldn't fight off the microbes. They simply latched on and bided their time. Thus, when I died, the little buggers revived my organs and then began to mutate my DNA. My musculature increased while my insides consumed the extra gut fat for fuel. There were other cellular changes that I couldn't quite understand.

Luckily, the nanites halted the mutation, ate the microbes, and then stabilized my system. If they hadn't, I might've woken up as a something instead of a someone. Just before I regained consciousness, the nanites spread throughout my body and then slipped into some kind of passive mode.

Fair enough.

As for the Black Wheel, I had to assume that these assholes had control of the ship, its sensors, and its weaponry. Once they realized I was up and around, they could come after me—or have the ship gun me down. Since I couldn't phase anymore, I had to be sneaky.

Then there was Grace.

Normally, I'd write her off. Today warranted an exception, though. Odds were that she was being taken directly to a Black Wheel higher-up—someone with the secrets I needed to know. Besides, saving her ass would annoy these sons of bitches, which made it the right thing to do.

I secured the wakizashi and then put both hands against a nearby (well-lit) wall, which gave me a small shadow to work with. I thought of Grace and opened a tiny shadow tunnel to her location –

Grace was screaming on the other side of it.

I put my eyes against the shadow and looked through. Drenched in sweat, Grace was strapped to a metal exam table via thick leather restraints. Based on the Cyrillic signs in the background, I knew she was on the Med Level (Deck Three). She looked on helplessly while a healer played with her insides. The lower part of her blouse was unbuttoned, allowing him to put his hands directly into her stomach.

Given time, Grace would talk because "torture-by-healer" was too awful a process to endure. The fucker could control her nervous system on a whim and prevent her from passing out or dying. He'd keep her in a physical hell until she cracked. Most people broke in under a minute. Clearly, Grace was made of sterner stuff.

From my low angle, I could see the tall man's pale face and dyed blonde hair. Close to his 50's, the fucker wore a less-militant style of Black Wheel field attire.

The black duster, white suit, white shirt, and matching bow tie suggested that he was management—someone in the know. Wrist-deep into Grace's body, the healer gave her a patient, sadistic smile.

"Where are they hidden, Grace?" The healer asked. "We know that some of the ArgoKnights are still alive. Some of their Support Staff had to have survived as well. Tell me how to find them and you'll suffer no longer."

"Go to Hell!" came her defiant reply.

"I see that you were pregnant once," he casually assessed. "A miscarriage, yes?"

Grace shuddered as she resolutely stared at the ceiling.

"That's a shame," the healer replied. "I think you should experience the full pain of childbirth—the sort of labor every mother dreads. A few hours of this and you'll be begging to talk."

That's when I nailed him.

Fuck it. I wasn't human anymore. Most newly-minted monsters would hold off on that first feed out of some useless sense of guilt. Honestly, I didn't mind surviving at someone else's expense—especially this asshole. Besides, after coming back from the dead, I needed a meal.

Anyway, I ripped him . . . sort of. A spirally tendril of black energy erupted from my right hand, went clean through my little shadow tunnel, and latched onto his back right leg. The shadow tendril solidified and quickly tangled him up in a black cocoon. Bound mouth-to-toe, the healer uttered a muffled yelp of surprised agony. His exposed hands slid out of Grace as he stumbled backwards and fell.

Now that I had my own "interface" to this motherfucker, I fed on him. I didn't just rip most of his life force away—his memories got sucked up too. The horribly-satisfying process was over in about eight seconds, followed by him convulsing on the floor. Grace looked down at me with horror as I climbed out of a nearby shadow.

"You're dead!" Grace gasped.

"And you scream like a girl," I muttered as I took my wakizashi and cut her loose.

She gingerly rolled off the table, putting it between us. Clearly in pain, the psi-hacker eyed the room's only exit, which was to her immediate left.

I had to laugh.

"You're not really thinking about running through this booby trapped ship, are you?" I sneered at her.

"W-What did you do to him?!" Grace asked.

My hunger sated, I simply shrugged and gave Grace a satisfied smile. Then I looked over at my first victim. Archibald Cramm (the mostly-dead healer on the floor) didn't look so good. Sweaty and pale, he started to bawl like an angry baby in a man's body.

"Poor Archie's mind just got looted. I ripped every memory in his head after the age of four months."

Under the bright overhead lighting, my shadow cocoon started to break down. Black mist steamed away from the tendrils and toward the nearest shadows. Apparently, bright light was a partial limitation of mine.

A bit woozy, Grace looked up from the crying healer.

"You gonna be okay?" I asked.

Grace shook her head.

"Then get back on the table. I'll fix you up."

"Says the freak with the blade," Grace grimaced . . . before she hopped back on the table.

"Now that we've re-established trust," I turned toward Archibald and 'jacked his shadow.

In my augment days, I used to love ripping shadowjackers. These supers could actually manipulate someone else's shadow and make it come to life for short periods. Most 'jackers were deadly motherfuckers; able to kill victims—with their own shadows—without even being in the same room. While I couldn't rip powers anymore, this was the next best thing.

I willed Archibald's shadow to slide out from under him. It stood up, turned solid, and then cracked its knuckles as it headed over to Grace.

"What are you doing?!" She balked.

"Turning off the pain and giving you full access to your powers," I informed her. "Archie here shut them off."

Grace shot the healer (and his shadow) an angry glare as she leaned back.

"Get it over with," she said.

The shadow construct plunged its hands into her stomach. Grace grimaced from the painful intrusion for a few seconds . . . and then calmed down. A hesitant grin formed on her face.

"Better?" I asked.

"Much," she admitted.

As the shadow did its thing, I focused on Archibald's memories and pulled up the relevant details.

"He came with a twelve-man team," I told her. "Find the remaining nine."

Archibald's shadow withdrew its hands and stepped back.

"All done," it replied with his voice (freaking both of us out).

"Thanks!" I patted its right shoulder. "Back you go."

The construct nodded, turned back into a regular shadow, and slid under the healer.

"Creepy, ain't it?" I grinned.

Grace rolled her eyes and looked up at the ceiling as she psi-hacked into the ship.

"Dumbasses didn't even bother to change the master code!" Grace shook her head with amazement.

Based on Archibald's memories, I knew that using the master code did indeed trigger a seven-minute delay. The delay was meant to give intruders a false sense of control. Any scouts would "secure" the ship and give an "all-clear" to the rest of their attacking force. By the time a breaching team(s) entered, their seven minutes would be up and the defenses would kick in.

"Changing the master code. Tapping into the sensors . . . now."

"Where are they?"

"They're in three-man teams, sweeping the ship for any other surprise guests," Grace explained. "By the way, I've got two armed submersibles coming in to pick them up. ETA: two minutes."

I pulled up Archibald's memories and then glanced at my watch. The bastards didn't plan on Grace psi-hacking the ship in-person. Instead, they had teams ready to trace her psi-hack and capture her.

"They were planning on taking you with them," I told her. "Once you were broken, you'd be brainwashed and forced to psi-hack for them."

Grace's disgusted reaction spoke volumes. She looked at my holstered handguns and held out her hands.

"Mind if I borrow those?"

I drew my Walthers and handed them over, butt-first.

"Thanks," Grace said as she tucked one into the back of her slacks. The other she held in her right hand.

"So, what's the plan?" Grace asked.

"Ever play *Battleship*?"

The psi-hacker shook her head, wishing she had thought of that.

"Activating external guns. Should I autogun the rest of Archie's team?" Grace asked.

Damn! Why didn't I think of that?

"If you would," I replied after a thoughtful pause.

The ship vibrated as its external energy cannons blasted away for a few seconds . . . and then stopped. Then there was the thundering of autoguns rattling on three different decks. After a few seconds, they stopped too. The ship was ours again.

I noticed Grace's frown.

"What?"

"This ship's still a threat," Grace said. "Shouldn't we sink it? Give it to the Navy or something?"

"Um . . . no," I replied with a smirk.

"After all they've done to you, you're gonna give them their ship back?!" Grace asked.

"Hell yeah! See, I know where 90 tons of stolen Povchenko weaponry is hidden and how heavily that shit's being guarded. The Russians have the manpower to retake those weapons and the expertise to safely transfer it."

I gestured outward and looked around.

"They're gonna need a place to store it," she reluctantly conceded.

"Still, you can leave all kinds of back doors in the system," I suggested.

"Fine," Grace sighed. "I'll make the call. Just not here."

"Fair enough."

I flipped off one of the examination room's two light switches, creating plenty of shadows.

"Don't forget to erase the sensor logs."

"Way ahead of you," Grace assured me—right before she popped a cap into poor old Archie. I winced from the loudness of the shot and then admired the hole she put in his right temple. The last of the shadow tendrils misted away, leaving only the dead healer.

Oh yeah. The microbes.

Seeing as she had shadowported a few times, I scanned Grace for signs of mutation. The goggles picked up traces of dead microbes in her system. Even while she was being tortured, her immune system had easily shredded them. I guess they were only a problem when you were dying or dead. I made a mental note to check on Forecast and the others—just to be on the safe side.

"Can we stop off at an IHOP?' Grace calmly asked. "I'm starving."

"My treat," I yawned as I opened a shadow tunnel and gestured for her to go through.

CHAPTER TWENTY

Grace drew stares as she practically inhaled a Belgian waffle, scrambled eggs, bacon, and a second glass of orange juice. The stares had something to do with the way she set my guns on either side of her plate. They were so scared of her that they ignored my blood-covered suit, goggled face, and even my magnet-clamped wakizashi.

I simply enjoyed a second cup of coffee and basked in the glow of an artificial morning sky. Once her meal was eaten, Grace looked up at me and set her utensils down.

"So what now?" she asked.

"I clean myself up, tie up some loose ends, and get my house in order," I replied.

"You're staying?!"

"It's home," I shrugged.

"If you want to disappear, I have connections; folks who can get you off the grid."

"Not my style," I said before taking a sip.

There were questions galore burning behind her eyes. I set the white coffee mug down.

"Just ask," I urged her.

"All right," Grace leaned forward with a low voice. "Who the fuck are these guys?! And why were they trying to destroy the city?"

"Before we start," I replied with a low, threatening tone, "I want to make sure that you understand that last night never happened."

Grace leaned back into her chair, read my expression for a moment, and then nodded.

"Your secrets are safe."

"And why's that?" I pressed.

"Because you'll kill me—or worse—if I sell you out."

We shared a mutual grin. Then it was back to the problem at hand.

"For a project this large, The Black Wheel never just has one objective," I explained.

"Why's that?"

"Their schemes are designed so that—technically—they can't ever truly lose."

That worried her (as it should).

"What were they after?"

"You were the prime objective," I said. "They leaked the threat about the warhead to Mockre, hoping to lure you out."

"Yeah, they wanted to brainwash me," Grace acknowledged. "That part makes sense. What doesn't is why they'd want all of my old contacts."

"It does if they wanted to finish what they started in February of 2011."

Her mouth tightened.

"They were behind *Clean Sweep*?!" Grace angrily hissed.

I nodded.

"That was Stage One. With the heroes gone, they were revving up Stage Two—wherein they'd kill every top-tier crook on the planet."

"Why?"

"Because we're the only ones left who could stop them from achieving Stage Three," I replied.

"And that would be?"

I leaned back into my chair, amused by the genocide that was about to unfold on an unsuspecting world. Pillar City's destruction was mere foreplay, compared to what was coming.

"You've heard of the 'richest 1%', right?"

"Anyone not living in a cave has, Cly!" Grace impatiently replied. "So?"

"The other 99% are pissed off. They're whining about the widening wealth gap. Of how the richest 1% have no moral rationale for seizing so much of the pie, while everyone else struggles to make ends meet."

"What's that got to do with The Black Wheel?!" Grace pressed.

"The Black Wheel represents that richest 1% . . . like an advocacy group—only with guns. They're independently-ran and financed, without favoring any particular family dynasty, government, or corporation. Their sole purpose is to keep the wheels greased so that the rich could get richer."

I sifted through the rest of Archibald's memories as I took another sip of coffee.

"They always stay ahead of global trends," I continued. "At some point, they realized that we were headed for an eventual, all-out class war. Someday, the 'have-nots' will rise up against the 'haves' on a massive scale."

"If the poor are such a threat, what's The Black Wheel's plan?" Grace asked.

"Simple. Kill the 99%. All seven billion-plus of them."

Grace went speechless for a while. I took a sip of my coffee and admired the curves on a passing waitress—

"That's insane!"

"Be the Devil's advocate and it's not," I countered. "All of this class strife is tied to unsustainable population growth, 'hate-the-rich' politics, dwindling resources, and simple human greed. If the rich keep getting richer, there will be less and less to go around. Think about it, Grace. It's already begun. Things'll get worse until, one day, the unwashed masses will dog-pile the rich and slaughter them wholesale."

"You're assuming they're right!"

"And you're assuming they don't have precogs," I smugly countered.

Grace frowned, probably thinking of Forecast and the value of her visions.

"Technically, they're taking over the world, right?"

I nodded, surprised that someone else hadn't beaten them to the punch by now.

"If done correctly, they'll have a near-vacant world to convert into their own private Utopia. For it to work, no one can see The Black Wheel's finger on the trigger. Also, they have to do it without the planet getting wrecked in the process."

"The Povchenko weapons," Grace muttered with widened eyes. "That's why they raided *The Red Gate?* They needed designer weapons of mass destruction?!"

I nodded, pleased that Grace was keeping up with me.

"With those weapons—especially the viral stuff—they could trim the herd without ruining the planet. Ballsy, eh?"

Grace looked blown away.

"The weapons theft was their second objective," I continued as I took a sip and then set my mug down. "Thanks to your warning, that one might fail too."

"You think the Povchenkos can move in fast enough to recover their stuff?" Grace asked.

"I dunno."

She allowed herself a hopeful grin.

"Well, we screwed up two of their schemes. That's not so bad."

Her grin went away as my face darkened.

"Their third objective was to destroy my firm."

Grace paused to consider that one.

"They saw your mercs as a potential threat?"

"Something like that," I replied. "On that score, they won. I'm merely a nuisance now. A bunch of my best people are dead or in hiding."

"You think they got to Ray?"

"I plan to find out," I evilly grinned.

"What else were they planning?"

"Destroying Pillar City was also a prime objective." I said.

"But why?" Grace pressed.

"The large mobs, free-flowing money, and large population of supers make this place a potential monkey wrench to their grand design. For Stages Two and Three to succeed, Pillar City's gotta go."

"Goddamn it, Cly!" Grace hissed. "How many schemes did they have cooking?!"

"Just one more," I sadly grinned. "They wanted Seamus O'Flernan dead."

Grace frowned. "He was a threat?"

"Seamus wasn't just a threat to The Black Wheel— he was also a member," I winked.

Grace chuckled her disbelief.

"Why would Seamus O'Flernan participate in a planetary genocide?"

"Who says he knew?" I explained as I picked up my mug. "The Black Wheel figured out that Mockre was an ex-ArgoKnight, which explains his psi-screens, by the way."

Grace's poker face slammed on, confirming the accuracy of my stolen memories.

"They tipped off Seamus, figuring that he'd have Mockre killed on-the-spot. They'd only warn him because?"

"Because Seamus was one of them," Grace sighed as she ran a nervous right hand through her hair.

"By the way," I continued, "they also knew about Ratiapp, who was former Support Staff. On *The*

Depravity, Ratiapp's two killers were Black Wheel assassins, tasked with snatching him up for torture. Luckily, he died first."

A deep sense of regret and hatred crossed her face. In that moment, it was clear that Grace had declared her own private war with The Black Wheel.

Too bad she couldn't win it.

"Get back to Seamus," Grace said. "When did he join them?"

"Almost ten years ago," I shrugged. "To him, they were simply another networking group of rich opportunists who swapped business contacts."

"So Seamus didn't know what they were up to?" Grace frowned.

"Not until he grabbed Mockre, who somehow convinced him of The Black Wheel's real intentions. Then Seamus freaked out and tried to hire me to kill them off."

As she paused to process all of this, I gulped down more coffee. Grace sighed and stared over at a laughing couple and their adorable little daughter.

She envied them. She feared for them.

"I need your help," she admitted.

"I know."

"I need them dead," she stated.

I raised an eyebrow.

"You trying to hire me?" I grinned.

"Name your price and I'll wire it to your EDR inside of a minute," the psi-hacker promised.

I stared past her for a moment.

"No," I replied. "I'm not a fixer anymore. Nor a contractor."

"What are you then?" She tensely asked.

"Good question," I replied.

We sat quietly as I finished my coffee.

"Take care of yourself, Grace," I grinned as I stood up and fished out my wallet. "Good luck saving the world."

Bothered that I was simply going to leave, Grace walked around the table and grabbed my arm.

"Please, Cly!" Grace begged. "You can't sit this out! Billions of lives are at stake!"

I pulled my arm free.

"Wrong. I will sit this out," I lied as I pulled out a c-note. "They've beaten me and they know it. I've died once today and it wasn't fun. I'm not going to end up like Ratiapp or Mockre. No thanks."

I hope my performance was convincing. The surrounding, nosy-assed witnesses would report our conversation to the cops. The feds (and the mobs) would pull footage from a nearby security camera that Grace had been too distracted to notice. Anyone with the footage—and a lip reader—would get an indirect, damned-convincing debrief on The Black Wheel.

I set my money on the table, picked up one of my guns, and paused to consider her long odds.

"You really want to stop them?" I sighed.

Grace nodded with puppy dog desperation in her eyes. I snagged a piece of bacon off some old guy's plate. As I watched him cower in terror, I thoughtfully chewed it up. It wasn't as tasty as human life—but not bad either.

"Grace," I chewed. "Stop thinking like a cop. Think like a bastard."

"Okay," she replied, not quite getting my point.

"To win, they have to reach Stage Three, right?"

"They're starting Stage Two now," Grace nodded, trying to keep up. "Which means that more big-name villains are about to get killed."

"You need to convince those villains of what's coming," I explained. "Show them what we averted.

Warn the mobs, extremist groups, drug cartels, dictators, and so on: any villain who needs the dumb masses to thrive is (technically) on your side. Point them at The Black Wheel and they'll do your killing for you—or at least, dodge assassination attempts. Either way, you'll slow them down."

"Anything else I should do?" Grace asked, bothered by the idea of helping villainous scum survive.

"Assume that The Black Wheel has eyes everywhere, including your outfit. Mockre and Ratiapp were blown. How'd that happen?"

Grace sighed at the thought of a mole among her remaining contacts.

"What else?" she asked.

"Isn't it obvious?" I asked as I leaned in close. "Knock 'em back to Stage One."

"But how?!" Grace asked as she waved her hands with frustration. "All the heroes are dead!"

"Then make some new ones . . . and fast."

With that, I left.

THE END

ABOUT THE AUTHOR

Marcus V. Calvert is a native of Detroit who grew up with an addiction to storytelling that just wouldn't go away.

His goal's to tell unique, twisted tales that people will be reading long after he's gone. For him, the name and the fame aren't important. Only the plots matter.

You can find his books on Amazon and/or follow him on Facebook.

His website is: **https://squareup.com/store/TANSOM.**

Made in the USA
Columbia, SC
26 September 2017